NOT YET
A WOMAN

NOT YET
A WOMAN

W.C. Child

Red Pen Enterprises, LLC

Red Pen Enterprises, LLC

ISBN: 978-1-7322609-0-0
epub ISBN: 978-1-7322609-1-7
MOBI ISBN: 978-1-7322609-2-4

Cover Design by Scott McWilliams
Image by R-Tvist/Shutterstock.com

Printed in the United States of America.

2018943671
Library of Congress Control Number

Red Pen Enterprises, LLC
Clarksville, TN 37043

www.wcchildbooks.com

ONE

Summers at Big Mama's

The warmth of the air let me know the time was fast approaching for the long awaited sojourn to my summer home in the country, otherwise known as Big Mama's house. For as long as I could remember, my summers were spent there exploring nature and experiencing all out bliss. I was a city girl and the freedoms of those times were the best times of my life. There was an insect party every night at the light pole as the moths, gnats and mosquitos faithfully congregated in groups that swirled around like the shaken particles in a snow globe. The crickets and the frogs didn't pass on their invitation. They used their unique sounds to make their presence known at the bottom of the pole with less than honorable motives in mind for some of the unfortunate party-goers.

The adventures at the country estate were exciting and endless. I explored nature from sun-up to sundown. I only stopped long enough to devour lunch as quickly as possible so that every opportunity for blissful freedom was realized. Sometimes, the aroma that accompanied me when I finally made it home was an unwelcome guest of honor. It caused Big Mama to turn up her nose and ask if I had let puppies in the house. She would walk around the room sniffing and looking under furniture before making her way back to me. She then proclaimed that no human should look that cute, but smell so badly. Each time she did that, I wrapped my arms around her and rubbed against her in an effort to share my malodorous essence. She would pretend to try to push me away before we both broke out in laughter after she told me I really needed a bath.

Bath time was very soothing for me. We had many conversations about things that were not as important as the time we spent in each other's presence. The steaming hot water, along with how she hummed while she gently washed my back, filled my heart with such peace and relaxation. I would stay in the water until it became cold and cloudy and my youthful fingers transformed into shriveled raisins. Those moments were always filled with laughter and kindness and served as one way of her showing me unconditional love.

No matter how much I expressed my objection, Big Mama always gave me chores to do around the house. At first I thought my sad face and exasperated sighs would release me from my duties. I quickly learned I should save my energy for the work. She explained that working built character and I needed some sense of what it would be like when I had a job and other grown-up responsibilities. I asked myself why she was telling me to worry about things in the future. I didn't have a job; I was a child. As if she read my mind, she said, "You won't be a tomboy all your life. One day you will have a job and a family of your own. You will need these foundational skills to be able to thrive as a woman."

I always enjoyed having breakfast with Big Mama. Each day I woke up to the smell of bacon and the aroma of coffee, her self-professed liquid luxury. It brought joy to my nostrils and jealousy to my empty stomach. Unlike my chores, she never had to prompt me more than once about breakfast. She filled my plate with heaps of nourishment and she enjoyed her toast and Folger's coffee. I always begged for a sip of her coffee. I was elated when she poured some of it on a saucer. The once black liquid was diluted with milk until it was nearly white. But I didn't care. I slurped the concoction from the saucer the same as she did from her cup. We each thoroughly enjoyed our portions. It was how we started most days. We both knew that once breakfast was over and my chores were finished, I wouldn't see her again until lunch. Still to this day, I don't start my day without a good cup of coffee; not just for the flavor, but for the fond memories it represented in my life.

Near the end of each summer visit, I always begged to spend one more week with Big Mama. Daddy never consented. He was immune to the sad faces and the whining that accompanied the requests. I wished I could have been given the opportunity to continue with that ritual one more time. I knew that was beyond the realm of possibility. Daddy was dead. He was never coming back. Our family had suffered a terrible loss. The broken spokes of our life tried to continue spinning as if no repair was needed. Eventually, the weight of our new reality became too heavy for us to move forward. We were stuck in a vortex of pain and uncertainty.

When my mother mentioned I was going to Big Mama's house for the summer, I was surprised. The emotions that accompanied the announcement made me both anxious and conflicted. My daddy just died three months earlier. While I wanted to go to my place of respite, I didn't want to leave my mother home alone. She had been so sad since my father was no longer there. All she seemed to do was cry. The house felt hollow and devoid of the peace and contentment that had engulfed the place we called home. How sobering it had been to have strangers come to announce that the cornerstone of our fortress had been ripped from our family's foundation. My parents had hopes and dreams for our family; a real house for them and a college education for me. They used those aspirations to map out their interpretation of how our lives should go, but life got in the way. Without warning and without permission, it imposed its will on us as it saw fit. It never gave us a second thought. Changes came so quickly that there was no time to think about what to do next. We just held on for dear life and fought to make the necessary adjustments to survive. One day we laid down in strength and the next night in weakness. Something softly whispered in our ears to stay down. My mother listened intently and heeded those words of defeat. She didn't have the strength to fight.

Right after my father died, my mother barely looked at

me or touched me. Sometimes I thought she couldn't stand the sight of me. She used to always say I looked just like my daddy. Those words always brought a smile to my face and joy to her eyes, but not after he died. When daddy went away, so did the hugs, kisses and the essence of us. Most of the time when she looked at me, she cried. Her troubled eyes said how much she missed my daddy, even though the words never made their way from her lips to my ears. I missed both of them.

I wasn't sure my mother really had a chance to mourn the death of my father. Because she had to take care of me, she couldn't unburden the broken parts of her soul. She tried to put on a brave face, etched with false smiles and vacant glances. She was far from the joyful soul who had made that building a home. It felt like she was stuck between two places and couldn't find the way out. The humming sounds she made when she prepared dinner for us were replaced by sniffles and dry commands when she announced dinner was ready. Most times she didn't eat anything at all and I was left to eat the family dinner alone. When she retreated to the confines of the bedroom, she never wanted to leave. Some nights I climbed in bed with her so she wouldn't be alone. She would hold on to me as if she was afraid to let go. During those times, I felt helpless. I secretly wished my daddy would walk through the front door one night so she could be happy again. But I knew that was not going to happen. I was there when they put him in the ground and covered his decorated box with dirt. He wouldn't be able to save her.

Little by little, my mother was fading away. I feared when I returned from Big Mama's house, all of the old her would be gone. Maybe she just needed some time alone without having to constantly worry about taking care of me. She could barely take care of herself. My gift to her that year could be a summer without me. If she had the time and space, she could recover from our loss and concentrate on getting better. Eventually her joy would return and she would learn to smile again. Surely it couldn't hurt. At that point, we were trapped in sorrow. We both wanted time to go backward to the happier days, but we knew that was impossible.

TWO

To Grandmother's House We Go

The drive to Big Mama's house was one of the things our family enjoyed the most. Daddy always committed to making the long trip an enjoyable one. We sang songs, told jokes, laughed and talked the entire time. I couldn't wait for him to look at me thru the rear view mirror and ask me if my stomach was ready. I knew what that meant; it was time to go over the big hill. Although he warned me every time, I never could control gravity's effects on my insides. Feelings of wonder and amazement caused my joy to infect our surroundings. Each time my parents laughed at my reaction.

Even though it was just the two of us, I expected the same ritualistic experience on the trip to Big Mama's house. I was disappointed when our route took us toward the ferry. The pathway that would have given me a chance to re-live some of the joyful memories I shared with my father was excluded from this trip. Maybe the shorter route was best for my mother. The normal route would have been littered with landmarks and memories too permanent to ignore. She would have been reminded of what could never be again.

The normalcy I longed for, that would keep the memory of my father alive in the confined space of the car, eluded me. There was no laughter, no joy and nothing that reminded me of the rituals my father and I shared. The longer we rode, the louder the silence of the non-verbal moments became. Out of desperation, I turned up the radio and allowed voices of faceless people and lyrics of songs I didn't know to keep me company for the remainder of the trip.

When we pulled up into the driveway, we tooted the horn to signal our arrival. As always, Big Mama and Big Daddy were there to greet us with open arms, warm hugs and genuine words of welcome. I was ready to get out of that car and finally have a conversation with someone who seemed to notice I was there. It was the first trip to my grandparent's house since my father's death. I wondered if my mother's sadness made the trip as well. Big Mama and my mother hugged each other and remained frozen in that position for an extended period of time. During their embrace, they shared tears and secret thoughts, even though no words were spoken.

Big Mama's house was filled with the life and the spirit of my father's early years. I worried about how my mother would react to all the reminders of his life. My mother spent time looking at pictures of my father that were distributed throughout the house. She touched places they shared during their love story. I watched her linger in several familiar spots as she tried to capture enough of his essence to sustain her a while longer. The more time she spent in the house, the sadder her eyes became. Shortly after dinner, she excused herself and withdrew to their old bedroom.

She bravely tried to spend the night in the room where they usually slept. By morning, she occupied the space in bed next to me. She appeared to have gotten little sleep and restoration never made it to her soul. Although she hugged me and tried to hide it, her weary face and eyes showed the aftermath of her tears. In those eyes, I saw the same sadness that had been there for the last few months. Maybe by being at Big Mama's for the summer, it would allow my mother time to find the way back to normal. I needed my old mother back.

I understood how difficult this trip had been for my mother. I was relieved when she informed us of her plans to leave. As was the tradition, hugs were shared by everyone as bags were placed in the car. When the time came for our embrace, my mother hugged me for a long time. After she released me, she looked into my eyes for an extended period of time. For a minute, I saw a glimpse of the mother I knew before my father died. Before the floodgate of awaiting tears could open, she flashed a smile, kissed me on the cheek and bravely made her way to the car. I waved goodbye to my mother for as long as I thought she could see me through the rear-view mirror. I quickly turned my attention to having the best time of my life. I decided to let the freedom of being in the country work its magic and replace any sadness with childish glee.

That summer vacation was all I thought it would be. I was able to just be a child and not the adult in the relationship. At home I felt lonely, even though my mother occupied the same space. I shared with Big Mama bits and pieces of our lives after my father passed. She sat quietly on the porch swing and let me talk as much as I needed. She carefully measured her words before commenting on my viewpoint.

We rocked back and forth on the swing for a minute then she said, "I don't mean to meddle, but the past few months have been very difficult for your mother. Your parents truly loved each other and were each other's better half. When you lose someone that special, it's not like losing a toy or money; those things can be replaced, but not people. We are only here for a brief moment and should be cherished as the true gifts we are."

Big Mama pulled me onto her lap and cradled me in her arms before she continued, "Saying good bye to someone you loved that much is harder than you can imagine. It hit your mother pretty hard. Now your mother just needs time to get back on track after experiencing such a great loss. She loves you and thought that the best gift she could give you was time with us. You needed more time and attention than she is able to give right now. I thanked her for putting you first. That is how much she loves you. Do you understand?"

"Yes ma'am."

"Good. I don't ever want you to forget that."

For the rest of the evening, we sat in the swing and further strengthened our bond. I loved Big Mama for her wisdom and for always taking care of me.

As the days got shorter, I knew my holiday was coming

to an end. At night as I sat on the porch swing, I marveled at the clear night sky and the brightness of the stars. I never saw the beauty of the sky in the city or any of the marvelous gifts of nature. I sat there and listened to the crickets and bullfrogs and watched the fireflies spread their temporary lightshow across the yard. I never got tired of those simple pleasures.

I was going to miss the temporary distraction from the harsh reality of my life in the city.

My mother would be coming soon and I was looking forward to our reunion. Big Mama talked to me several times over the course of the summer. Each conversation was filled with advice about how to conduct myself when I went back home. The thoughts of what awaited me filled me with mixed emotions. I hoped my mother had used our time apart to heal, but there was no guarantee. I wanted so much for us to be like we were before our family tragedy. I missed the closeness we once shared and looked forward to things getting back to normal. Memories of my father invaded my mind and I was forced to remember that he would never be there again. When I returned to the family home, our entire family would not be there. The time spent with my paternal grandparents helped fill the void created by the loss of my father. They needed me to remind them of how life goes on beyond our losses. All of our tanks had been refilled enough for the next phase of our attempts to overcome the things lost over the past few months. I was ready to go home.

THREE

Grown Folks' Business

I was supposed to be asleep, but I wasn't. I just had my head buried deep under the covers with my back turned to the door when I heard it open. Big Mama was checking in on me, so I made snoring noises to convince her I was resting peacefully. At night after I went to bed, she always had private telephone conversations. I often wondered why she waited until I was not around for those exchanges. Some nights, those guarded exchanges were speckled with snickering, chuckling and out right laughter.

One day I was foolish enough to ask Big Mama about the content of one of those conversations. That question exposed me to a side of her that I had only heard about from my father. I saw the "evil eye". According to him, she could put fear into your heart with just one look. Not only did I see it, I felt the effects of it. He was right. Big Mama captured my full attention with that evil eye and I got scared. It felt like I was being hypnotized. I was unable to break away from the mesmerizing trance. When she spoke, I didn't recognize the voice that made its way to my ears. Her voice dropped an octave and the words tumbled out of her mouth in slow motion. I half expected her eyes to pop out of their socket and her head to spin around. She promptly told me that I should stay out of grown folks' business. I knew, without a doubt, not to ever ask that question again.

Since the direct information gathering method was not an option, I devised another way to hear what was so special about grown folks' business. One night I decided to test my bravery and venture into enemy territory. I was determined to satisfy the curiosity beast that taunted me most of the summer. I eased my way down the hallway toward Big Mama's bedroom door. From the sound of her voice, which constantly went from firm to soft and sometimes faded away, I knew I was about to hear something really good. The closer I got to the door, the more I implored the creaky wooden floors to cooperate with me. If my plan worked, I could hear all of the juicy grown folks' business I wanted.

I stopped just shy of the door and crouched down in a spot where I could hear Big Mama's voice.

Big Mama was not happy when she said, "Come again. You want us to do what?" I was happy until I heard her say, "You want us to keep her until Christmas? No, I don't think we can do that. What about school?"

I took a deep breath and continued to listen. Big Mama said, "You're moving? Moving where? Why are we just hearing about this? You've had plenty of time to tell us before now. And now you want me to tell her you're not coming to pick her up."

I could tell how upset Big Mama was when her elevated voice responded, "I heard you, but now I want you to hear me. More than ever, she's got to come first. Her daddy ain't been dead six months and your child needs you. This ain't right, and you know it. I know this is gonna break her heart more than it already is."

Big Mama was right. My heart was breaking with each revelation I uncovered with my eavesdropping. I was lost in those thoughts until I heard Big Mama say, "I know he was my child, just like she is yours. I know how hard this is. But I still say, y'all really need each other right now. Ain't no man worth sacrificing the relationship with your daughter. If that's what he's asking you to do, he ain't worthy of your time. I don't know why you can't understand that."

The floors responded to Big Mama's movements. Then she said, "What else can we do? You didn't leave us much choice. Your decision was made long before you called. Let's just hope you won't live to regret this."

After Big Mama said goodbye, she took out her frustration on the phone's cradle. The bed moaned from the weight of her body and possibly the conversation with my mother. There was silence and then I heard her cry out, "Please help her Lord Jesus!" I didn't know if she was talking about me or my mother.

I crept silently to my bedroom, got back in bed and tried to understand the gravity of what I just overheard. I knew it really was grown folks' business they had discussed. I felt so alone in that moment. I tried to figure out how their plans would truly impact my life. Decisions were made for me, but my feelings were not considered. How I felt didn't seem to matter. Had anyone asked, I would have chosen to go back home. My mother needed me; we needed each other. We were all that was left of our nuclear family. Since my father and I would no longer be there, three plates were no longer needed for the kitchen table. One plate would be enough. I needed to tell my mother that If she let me come back home, I wouldn't cause her any trouble. I would help around the house, just like big Mama had told me to do. I just wanted to be with my mother.

The tears began slowly and quickly picked up speed. Before long they streamed down my face like the raindrops that connected to the window pane, fell prey to gravity and were forced to find another resting place. I felt lost and confused. I questioned why my mother didn't want me anymore. Not only that, she didn't have the decency to talk to me about it. She left that task to Big Mama. I feared it wouldn't be long before she would forget about me altogether. Had I known I would not be going back home, I would have never agreed to go to Big Mama's that year. As I sat in the quietness of my dark room, I felt like the forgotten toy nobody claimed from the lost and found.

The light of the new day filtered through the curtains and I fought to gain control of my emotions. I dreaded the news that was in store for me. I lingered in my room until I heard Big Mama call me down for breakfast a second time. In order to conceal last night's "mission", I had to pretend I knew nothing about my mother's decision. Throughout the night, I prayed through sniffles and tears that my mother changed her mind about leaving me with my grandparents.

I hoped she had called back and told Big Mama when she would be there to pick me up. I whispered another brief prayer and reluctantly went downstairs.

I followed my normal breakfast routine, but Big Mama didn't. When I asked for coffee, she agreed immediately. I knew then that my prayers had not been answered. My fate had been sealed. My soul ached from the unexpected loss of both of my parents. Big Mama did her best to explain how my staying with her a little bit longer was best. She explained that my mother needed more time for herself and I needed the stability remaining with her and Big Daddy would bring. Had I not been eavesdropping the previous night, I would have been convinced it was her idea. We both knew no other options were available. Big Mama's house was my new home.

At first I felt like a grown-up when Big Mama shouted I had a phone call. Those lifelines from my mother always lifted my spirits and made me feel wanted. She was always in a good mood and appeared glad to talk to me. Maybe that was a sign she was getting better. When our conversations neared the end, I sometimes asked my mother to send me something. The things I asked for were not out of greed. They were just a way to constantly have pieces of her that would tide me over until we were reunited. I really didn't care about what she sent. I just needed something to demonstrate I still mattered.

After a few months, the phone calls from my mother declined until I only heard from her on special occasions, like Christmas, Easter and my birthday. I often wondered if she missed me as much as I missed her. I didn't know for sure. She always promised presents and visits, neither of which materialized. Maybe that's why the calls dwindled into nothingness; she couldn't afford to send anything and didn't want me to be disappointed. I vowed not to ask for anything the next time she called. I just wanted to hear her voice.

I constantly pestered Big Mama about the mail and whether a box finally came for me. To mask my disappointment, I used my imagination to make up stories of inept mailmen who delivered my beautiful gifts to the wrong address. It was all I could do to avoid the truth. My mother was long on words, but short on action. I wasn't sure if I was angry or relieved when the phone calls stopped. At least I didn't have to deal with the sadness that was wrapped up, tied in a nice bow, and placed in empty gift boxes that never arrived. I wanted to think she still loved me and cared about what was happening to me, but I had no conclusive evidence. Based on outcome, I didn't matter much. Maybe she still needed a little more time to stop being sad. In the meantime, I would have to be content in my temporary home and with Big Mama's attempt to fill in where my mother fell short. The replacement gifts I got from Big Mama undoubtedly were bought at the dollar store. At the time, I didn't understand the sacrifice they made on my behalf to provide something for me when my mother broke another promise.

Eventually, I realized the long distance relationship

with my mother became more about wishes and promises and less about retaining us as a family unit. With each broken promise came another crack in the foundation of who I thought we were. Two more summers passed and still no sign of my mother. I had begun to think this would be my permanent home.

FOUR

The Talk

Over the next two years I spent with Big Mama, I saw changes in my body that I didn't welcome. Along with those changes came new instructions about other growing up topics I was not interested in discussing. She already made me wear a contraption called a training bra. I didn't grasp the concept behind the necessity of that clothing item. The small mounds on my chest were just there. They didn't move, so I didn't understand what about those things needed to be trained. And why in this world would a boy ever want to look at or touch them? It was all foreign to me, but if that was what I had to wear to get outside to play, I would be foolish to object. At times I chuckled when I saw Big Mama's bra hanging beside mine on the clothes line. It was almost like comparing sling shots to cannons. I shuddered to think about what these things would look like once the training was over. Please God, don't let there be cannons in my future!

Just when I thought I had experienced all the growing up I could handle in one summer, I was dealt another devastating blow. In my mind, my life as I knew it was over. Every day we planned some new excursion and that day was no different. We were headed to the railroad tracks to look for souvenirs, but before we got too far, I thought I cut my leg. I had to go back home. To my surprise, Big Mama looked for, but could not find, the cut I needed to cover. Suddenly her expression changed and I saw a different look in her eyes. Then, out of the blue, she hugged me. I didn't know what was going on. I knew it was bad when she told me to sit down because we needed to talk.

I wasn't ready for that conversation. I was bombarded with a series of contradictions that rivaled any fairy tale I ever heard. When she told me how babies were made, I thought for sure she exaggerated the facts. Her persistence convinced me it was all true. Until then, I never thought about where babies came from. I thought that, like everything else, they were bought from somewhere, and in this case, the hospital. However, I remembered the day those two dogs were stuck together out in the yard. My friends and I laughed at how ridiculous they looked. Big Daddy turned a water hose on them until they separated and ran away. Big Mama told me that people got stuck together like that too. Since people outnumbered dogs, there must be water hoses at everybody's house. I tried to remember if I had seen one at their house. Sure enough, there was one outside. Good thing I never saw Big Mama and Big Daddy stuck together. I wasn't sure I could have sprayed them with a water hose.

I didn't understand why she chose that day to tell me all that stuff. I only went into the house for a band-aid. The next thing I knew, I had a list of do's and don'ts and nevers and can'ts that I couldn't process. My mind was pre-occupied with getting back outside. I didn't care about her euphemisms related to pocketbooks and change and other nonsense beyond my current comprehension level. I had no treasure to protect and I didn't carry a pocketbook. Any change I had was liberated by the five and dime or the closest candy or toy store as quickly as I got it in my hands. I couldn't grasp what any of it had to do with boys. It was like she was talking in code. I already knew to stay away from bird's nests and beehives, but her correlation between those things and my current minor medical situation was lost in translation.

The longer we talked, the worse the news became. Big Mama told me I bore the responsibility of procreation. Since I had entered womanhood, I was able to reproduce babies. I didn't want that chore. I questioned why this fell on women. My heart sunk when she told me I would have a crimson-colored visitor every month. I didn't want to hear any more. That misfortune was one I wouldn't be quick to embrace. I picked a bad day to need a band-aid.

As I rode with Big Mama to the drugstore, I thought about the information overload I had just encountered. I questioned how those things were fair to women. If I had my way, things would be different. I would put more reproduction responsibilities on the male species. The boys would have to suffer through the whims of Mother Nature's monthly inconveniences and donate their bodies for incubation duties for nine months. Maybe then, there would be fewer babies and there wouldn't be a need for as many water hoses.

FIVE

Decision Made

I didn't hear Big Mama use that voice very much, but when she did, I knew she meant business. I felt sorry for the person on the other end of that phone call until I figured out the subject of the conversation was me.

"I understand, but I can't do it no more. She's growing up and I don't think I can handle this too much longer. I've had this child with me for the last three years. It's time for you to take care of your own responsibilities." Big Mama tried several times to interject, but had to wait until my mother finished her end of the conversation.

"I think you've forgotten how much it costs to raise a child since you haven't done it in a while. I can hardly keep her fed, not to mention buying her shoes and clothes. You don't even know what size she wears now. That should tell you something." Big Mama paused. When she spoke again, her voice's volume conveyed how irritated she was with my mother's response.

"You need time? Time for what? It's been three years. How do you think your baby feels? She barely knows you now because you hardly talk to the child anymore." I nodded my head in agreement with Big Mama's comment. The floors continued to squeak as she paced back and forth. If she wandered into the hallway, I was dead.

Big Mama was angry when she responded, "Watch it now. You don't want to bring my son's name up in this mess. This is all you. I bet he is rolling over in his grave because of what you're doing to his child. No matter how you look at it, this ain't right and you know it."

There was a really long silence and I wanted to peek inside the room before I heard Big Mama say, "I'm sure you do love her, I don't doubt that, but that's not all there is to it. You've got to be present in her life to show her that you love her. Like I said, you've got to start helping out financially with the raising of YOUR daughter."

Things were not going well for my mother. I almost felt sorry for her, but I didn't. Big Mama had said a lot of things that were true. She continued to talk to my mother about her financial responsibilities. "Get it from where? I already tried that. They told me you getting it all. They said you been getting it way before you dropped her off at my house three years ago."

Big Mama responded bluntly, "Now that's what they told me. I certainly believe them over you. They ain't got to lie. They don't get the money, you do."

Big Mama quickly asked, "So who's getting the check? You gotta be getting it. She sure ain't. She ain't seen a nickel of it. I'm gonna need you to start sending something our way. It ain't right that we here struggling and you're good-timing your, naw, I meant to say, her money away.

You ought to be ashamed of yourself. I tell you what, either you start sending something here or pick her up at the Greyhound bus station."

The last thing I heard Big Mama say before scampering back to my room was, "Try me. You got two weeks!"

My final snooping expedition was the best one ever. I sneaked around and listened to more grown folks' business between Big Mama and my mother that unexpectedly ended in my favor. When I returned to my room, I was ecstatic. I circled the date on the calendar and anxiously waited for the ultimatum deadline to pass. Big Mama was true to her word. Three weeks after the school year ended, she announced that I was going back to my mother. I pretended to be both shocked and saddened by the announcement. My performance could have garnered an Academy Award. It was that good; as good as my information gathering missions that had gone undetected.

At last I was finally going to be reunited with my mother. It was long overdue. As I sat on the Greyhound bus headed for my long awaited family reunion, it was hard to control myself. I fought the urge to scream for joy. I was happy to say bye to Big Mama's house and all those crazy rules I thought made no sense. And if I heard one more thing about protecting my "pocketbook", I would have screamed.

Although I had unlimited happiness about ending one phase of my life and embarking on another, I experienced unexpected fear about our family's impending reunification. It had been a long time since I made eye contact with my mother. I was afraid I wouldn't remember what she looked like. The one family picture I still possessed became faded and torn over the years. I often placed it in bed with me to feel close to my parents. The picture captured a moment in time when we were all together and the love we had for each other spoke loudly from behind the glossy sheen. That still-life treasure would once again occupy a place of prominence in our home, just as it had before our family fell apart.

Screeching tires and the sight of people gathering their belongings indicated I had finally reached my destination. From the window of the bus I could see a crowd of people inside the terminal waiting to greet passengers whose travels ended at that station. People rushed to the arms of those anticipating their arrival and shared extended hugs and smiles. No one appeared to be there to share that type of warm welcome with me. Panic overtook my joy. I worried my mother forgot about me once again. Big Mama gave me instructions and phone numbers in case no one was there to meet me. I prayed I wouldn't have to use them. Doing so would confirm I wasn't important enough for my mother to take the time to welcome me home.

My eyes wondered past her, then back, before I settled on her face. A wave of relief wrapped me in warmth after our eyes met and she waved at me. It took me a while to fully recognize the person she had become. From the look in her eyes, it appeared the feeling was mutual. I had not imagined a marching band, but I expected a more genuine greeting than the one I received. After being apart for over three years, I wanted her to act like she was glad to see me. I expected my mother to jump up and down with glee and cover my face with kisses like they did on those TV shows. But instead of that kind of reception, the look in her eyes and the seemingly forced smile showed both happiness and fear. The image of the little girl she preserved in her mind from three years earlier had changed. I had developed in places I didn't know existed. Because of the way her eyes scanned my body, I almost felt embarrassed about the person I had become. I had blossomed into a young lady who had budded and rounded out in so many places. I may have looked like my daddy, but I was built like my mother, curves and all.

After years of freedom in the country, I returned to the confines of city living. Concrete sidewalks, street lights and noise replaced seemingly endless amounts of green grass, dark nights that cheerfully exposed the stars, and open places to roam. Not that I didn't appreciate being with my mother, but Big Mama's house became much more appealing once I stood inside my new home. I thought it would at least be of the same caliber as the home we shared with my father, but it was far from it.

I sat my suitcase beside the sofa and took a closer look at my surroundings. My first impression was that the place felt tired and in need of what Big Mama called "a good cleaning" to get rid of the stench that immediately filled my nostrils. Dirty dishes were piled in the sink under cold dishwater that recycled the scent of yesterday's food. The contents of the small garbage can exceeded its height and needed the wall to balance the excess. The layer of dust camped out on the tables confirmed that not much attention was paid to those every day chores. The strong odor of stale cigarette smoke made the room smell like an ashtray. The aroma was far from the familiar welcoming smell that cheerfully wafted from Big Daddy's pipe.

As I walked down the hallway toward the bedroom, I scanned my surroundings looking for some recognizable link to our family's once happy life. I was looking for something to trigger hope within me that the apartment could somehow be transformed into a home. To my surprise, I saw no photos of the family life we shared. There were no pictures of me either. It was as if that place had no idea I even existed until I made my physical presence known. I didn't understand. I was sure Big Mama sent her pictures of me. Where was I? Big Mama took pride and great care in finding the right frame to honor my pictures. They were spread throughout the house. I thought my mother would do the same. Since they weren't anywhere else, I was confident my pictures were nicely framed and on the bedside table with those of my father's. We would be the first faces my mother saw in the morning and in the moments before she went to sleep. When we reached the bedroom, I found nothing. There were no frames, no photos and no family on display. It was hard to mask my disappointment.

My thoughts were interrupted when my mother instructed me to place my clothes in the hall closet. I was confused. I thought I would have my own room, or at the least, we would share the bedroom. I wanted to know why. It didn't take long for the "Why" to walk through the front door. My questions were answered when I heard the front door open and a deep male voice proclaimed, "Baby, I'm home."

It startled me when the sound of a male voice echoed down the hallway. I never considered there would be another person, especially not another man, sharing a home with my mother. Although logic dictated otherwise, I felt she was being disloyal to my father by being with another man. I was not ready to accept that she wanted to share her life with any man the same way she did with my father. My heart sank. I began to think both my father and I had been replaced. That man's presence probably explained why no visual reminders of our family were there.

Right before I boarded the bus, Big Mama talked to me about how important it was for us to rebuild our mother/daughter relationship. We needed to lean on each other for support until we were stable again. Apparently, she had found another support system. I started to get angry when I thought about how I was left for so long with Big Mama while she restarted her life without me. As if she sensed my confusion, she nervously grabbed me by the hand and ushered me down the hall to meet the person who interrupted our reunion.

The first glances between the three of us created a game of ocular ping-pong. Each of us was involved in our own version of the game. My mother looked nervous, I looked unsure and he looked too long. Not only did he look me in the eyes, he looked at my body in a way that made me feel uncovered. Although I couldn't define it right away, I saw what I later realized as the look of evil in his eyes. Meeting my father's replacement did not leave me with a good feeling in my core. I did not believe we could become a family.

With the introductions out of the way, my mother and her mate retreated to the bedroom. I was left standing in the space I realized would be my bedroom. By default, the convertible couch became my bed. My mother's bed was full. I was concerned that I would be afforded no sense of privacy. After looking into the creepy eyes of that stranger, I knew getting my own room had to be a priority.

It didn't take long for me to realize I couldn't remain out in the open for very long. One night I saw that man standing over me after I repositioned myself on the couch. It frightened me. Consequently, I became relentless in my quest to get my own room. I constantly reminded my mother of her promise to get a two-bedroom apartment. She promised we would move soon, but soon never arrived. I didn't get the family or the reunion I envisioned.

SIX

The Chase

The new living dynamic was less than ideal for me. I had never lived around any males who were not my blood. I didn't like my mother's boyfriend and never pretended that I did. I always had the feeling I was being watched. I would look up to find his intrusive eyes gazing in my direction. I felt I was being hunted. I didn't like that feeling. Something about that man was not right. His mere presence consumed the air I breathed. I made it a point to keep my distance from him.

He tried too hard to gain my trust. I ignored his attempts. I knew I couldn't afford to let my guard down. Just the thought of him made my skin crawl. I had never experienced feeling uncomfortable in my own skin before. I had to be totally covered from head to toe, no matter how hot it got in that small apartment. My perception of his motives made me uneasy. I thought he was trying hard to get glimpses of those sacred places that Big Mama taught me to protect. I had prepared my mind for unwanted attention from pubescent males whose voices changed from deep to screechy from one sentence to the next. Never had I imagined that type of negative attention from a man who was old enough to be my father.

To my discomfort, it seemed he was always around. When I left for school, he was there. When I came home from school, he was there. I was sure no job in America had such great work hours. But for someone with no apparent source of income, he was never without alcohol or cigarettes. He and my mother always found ways to satisfy vices at the expense of other necessities.

I remember the day he first tried to hug me. He grabbed my wrist and told me to give my "new daddy" a hug. I quickly pulled away from his grasp. He laughed and told me I looked like a deer caught in the headlights. He took another draw on the cigarette that hung loosely from his mouth and winked at me. A chill ran through my body. I told him he was not my daddy and to never touch me again.

As I headed for the apartment door I heard him laugh and say, "Where you going? You can stay here with me. I'm not gonna bother you." He paused, exhaled the smoke and said, "You don't have to be scared of me. I'm yo new daddy and you're my sweet baby girl. I ain't gonna let nothing happen to you."

Horrible sounds of laughter exploded from an evil place I had no intention of getting to know. I quickly ran out the front door. I was too afraid to look back. His looks and innuendoes were not those of any "daddy" I wanted to know. I stayed away from that apartment until I knew my mother was home from work.

I was afraid all the time at a place that was supposed to be my home. I was sure he liked the fear he saw on my face every time he got close enough to rub my arm or touch my face. It was all part of his sick game. He enjoyed playing with me like a cat plays with a ball of yarn. I couldn't count the number of times he tried to brush up against me as we passed in the hallway. I feared it would be just a matter of time before something bad happened to me at the hands of this self-professed pseudo-daddy.

When I first arrived at my mother's house, she promised we would move to a two bedroom apartment. I needed privacy and a door that locked. I was still sleeping on the couch. I had no way to escape those eyes that were always looking for an opening. Although the bathroom became my sanctuary, it wasn't always the safe haven I so desperately needed. One night, the creaky bathroom door provided an alarm system that rivaled ADT when it alerted me the door was opening. The shower curtain concealed my body from the prying eyes and the unexpected surge of cold air. I was exposed, both mentally and physically. I quickly wrapped myself with a towel and rushed toward the bathroom door. To my horror, he stood motionless in the shadow of the hallway while he peeked through the crack in the door. After I slammed the door shut, my body trembled as I clutched my towel. I had always been so careful to ensure the door was locked, but not that time. He was getting too bold; too close. I had to make my mother understand that I needed to get my own room. Then at least I could lock my bedroom door and have some privacy. I needed a peaceful night's rest without worrying about what stage of the plan he was at. I knew I was in danger. I had to tell my mother everything.

SEVEN

Relief

Saturday was the one day I didn't have to fear the unwanted advances from my mother's boyfriend. Although we mostly ran errands and did laundry, I didn't complain. It was our private time together. During those times, I tried to squeeze out as much joy as possible. I needed to enjoy it while I could. I knew it would evaporate the minute I returned home where probing eyes and lecherous intentions overshadowed my hope for a peaceful existence.

I didn't know how to find the words to tell my mother the truth about the man she laid down with every night. Even though he had her, he wanted something from me too. From all accounts, she loved that man and lived with him like she did with my daddy. But unlike when she was with my daddy, she didn't laugh as much. She looked tired and sad. I was conflicted. I didn't want to add any more trouble to her already dismal life by telling my truth. After all, she abandoned me at Big Mama's house because of some man. If it came down to a choice between me and him, I wondered if she would choose me. It was too risky for me to find out right now. Instead, I decided to ask her if she was happy that I came.

When our eyes met, I saw hers were welling up with

tears. She struggled to find the words to express things that had been bottled up in her spirit for years. They were ready to make their exit. My mother composed her thoughts and cleared her throat before she said, "Of course I am. You're my baby. I missed you. All I've ever wanted was for you to be happy and safe. For a while, your Big Mama's house was the best place for you. But now, it's my time to take care of you again."

Her response made me happy. She took my hand in hers before she said, "The love of a mother can't be understood by most men. They don't understand how deeply we love and how hard we will fight for our children. You probably don't understand now why I left you with your Big Mama, but you will when it comes to your own children. As long as you are with me, I will never let anyone hurt you. That's my job as a mother; to always protect my child, without exception, without hesitation."

My mother gently pulled me into her arms and began to shower me with hugs and kisses. We both laughed as she squeezed me tightly into her breast. I closed my eyes and tried to recapture the feelings of days long ago. I thought about the times when daddy was alive and we were a happy family. When I opened my eyes, I expected to still see the lightness in her demeanor. What I saw was liquid sadness. I witnessed the gap narrow between joy and pain. Her emotions swiftly moved from one extreme to the other. As quickly as the sparkle and affection in her eyes appeared, it disappeared. I couldn't bring myself to tell her about what was going on with her boyfriend. She seemed to need protection as much as I did. I didn't want to hurt her, so I vowed to always know how to escape my danger.

I couldn't stand to see my mother with so much pain in her eyes. This was supposed to be a happy occasion. It was just the two of us hanging out together. We had to have some fun before we went back to our real lives. After we loaded the laundry into the car, I asked my mother if we could go to the arcade at the end of the block. It could definitely provide a temporary cure for our blues. We had enjoyed going to the fair as a family and although the arcade didn't offer the same activities, I convinced my mother that it would be really fun. We both enjoyed a carefree afternoon with each other. It had been a long time since I had seen this side of my mother. I longed to see more of that person. Before we left the arcade, we took several pictures in the photo booth. We both laughed at the images we captured. Maybe the pictures could begin the process of layering our relationship with new memories.

All things considered, it was a good day. I felt we were beginning to find our way back to each other again. Out of jealousy, I wondered how much closer we could be if she didn't have to split her attention between me and that man. When we turned the corner that led to our house, my demeanor changed. The relief I felt was short-lived. The freedom I felt with just having my mother around turned to fear as we got closer to our home. All the momentum I gained vanished when she put the car in park. It was time for me to transition myself from child to armed guard.

EIGHT

Game Over

T he night for me had been peaceful. I had the place all
to myself and was able to relax my mind. I had been
extra careful about being alone with my mother's boyfriend.
Since there had been no overt advances made toward me
lately, I honestly believed he finally dismissed me from his
mind. He and my mother had gone out earlier. If that Saturday night was like all the others, they would stumble in
around two o'clock. They would remain in their room until
well past the time when we should have been in somebody's
worship services. Just like clockwork, they made their less
than subtle entrance. I rolled over with my back facing the
door. I fooled Big Mama many times with that move and
didn't think twice about maintaining that posture after I
heard their bedroom door close.

At first I didn't know if I was asleep or awake. The
warmth of my blanket was replaced by the sudden chill of
cold air. I didn't have time to scream before the full weight
of his body was on mine. One of my arms was pinned
against the couch. With my free hand, I tried to pry from
my mouth and part of my nose those unwanted fingers of
the monster that had descended from Hell upon me. I strug-

gled with all my might to dislodge him from the superior position he commanded over me. My struggle was in vain.

Unwelcome sounds and smells overtook my senses. They were like nothing I ever experienced. He hungrily licked my face; I nearly gagged. The smell of his breath was a mixture of dirty ash trays, food and alcohol. His fingers viciously probed me in areas reserved for a sacred union. My eyes reacted in response to every intrusive thrust. My breathing increased in anticipation of the next agonizing sensation. I had to get him off me. I could not let him steal my bodily innocence. It could not be his victory. But the harder I struggled to release myself from his clutches, the stronger his determination grew to invade my inner space.

Pain ripped through my body in waves from places deep inside. I was engulfed in activities far too severe for a child who didn't fully understand her body's definition of womanhood. The sounds of fear and anguish that escaped from my throat were overtaken by the rhythmic grunting, snorting and guttural noises he made. He paid no attention to the constant wave of tears that saturated the edges of fingers that imprisoned my sounds. All I could think about was the pain. It continued long after I realized he completed his purpose. An awkward feeling of relief flooded my body when his movements stopped and he lay motionless in a heap on top of me. My naïve mind knew enough to understand the pain in my body would be worse if he started moving on me again. I held my breath and prayed for continued relief.

Silence returned to the room, broken only by his heavy breathing and the steady buzzing sound of the refrigerator. While his hand still covered my mouth, he delivered his final show of force. He put his mouth close to my ear and whispered, "If you tell your mother about this, I will kill both of you. Do you understand?" I nodded in submission. After he lifted the weight of his body from mine, he grinned and smugly exposed a perverted superior look in his eyes. He had conquered parts of my body and bits of my soul. As quietly as he appeared, he disappeared back down the hallway and returned to the bed of my mother.

The stillness of the room returned, but the screaming in my mind became louder. I tried to make myself invisible in the corner of the tattered sofa that had just been a battleground. I sat there motionless and defeated. He had launched his planned attack on my purity and staggered away with the spoils. My immaturity led me to believe I could control the actions of someone more cunning than I gave him credit for. I knew my innocence had died and my life would never be the same again.

NINE

The Aftermath

I gingerly removed my body from the crime scene and made my way toward the bathroom. It was the only place in the house where I felt safe. Each awkwardly painful step I made confirmed the end of my virginity. The smell of the act still lingered in my nostrils. All I wanted was to remove any form or substance of his existence from my body. Any reference to the sights and sounds of my attacker only accented and confirmed the destruction caused by his brutal entry. I always found a hot bath soothing and I needed all the comfort I could find. Maybe the cleansing of my natural body would restore some sort of sanity to my mind.

I eased myself down into the steaming hot cauldron of water. The hot water burned like alcohol on an open wound. I struggled to allow myself to remain fully submerged. There I wept openly and freely. In that private place, no one else heard the sounds of my anguish. Tears and mucus joined hands and plunged deeply into the steamy water. I stayed in the water until all the heat evaporated and my hands took on the consistency of prunes. I needed time and space to think about what happened. I needed the protection the small confined space provided. The once hot water both cleansed and started the healing process for my physical body, but my mental state required so much more time than the bathtub offered.

When I looked at myself in the mirror, I still saw the face of my old self, but on the inside, I no longer had an identity I recognized. I didn't know who I was any more. It took less than five minutes to change forever the essence of my being. I had no choice but to accept the consequences of someone else's inhumanity. My immediate goal was to survive that night with as much of myself in tact as possible.

I kept going over everything again and again in my mind. I tried to figure out what I had done to deserve his abuse. I found no answer. I knew I would never find an answer. His actions were beyond the reach of my inexperienced mind. I wondered how that temporary act could cause anyone to violate an innocent child against their will. I didn't even fully understand what just happened. It was nothing like what I had taken away as fact from the talks I had with Big Mama. She had not prepared me for that set of circumstances. I wondered what would happen next, now that round one had gone to the aggressor. I had few options available to protect myself. I was easy prey; always out in the open and never far from sight of the hunter.

I didn't know what awaited me beyond the bathroom door. If he was anywhere close by, my screams would be loud enough to wake everyone in the apartment building. I put my ear to the door to detect any sounds or movements from beyond. Slowly I cracked the door. I was chilled by the fresh air that rushed to engulf my freshly cleaned body. It was hard to determine if the chill I felt was because of the air or from fear. I breathed a sigh of relief after my eyes and my senses gave me the all clear sign.

Slowly I made my way back to the makeshift bedroom. I stood in front of the sofa and looked at the spot where I was violated. There was no way I would allow myself to touch the spot where I just lay in defeat. I violently flipped the cushions on the couch. I didn't want to be face to face with the shame of the recent violation. Although I was both mentally and physically exhausted, I found it impossible to entertain the thought of sleep. My senses remained on high alert. I couldn't close my eyes for fear of a second attack. I curled up in a ball and waited for daylight to come.

Tears flowed again. I was broken. I needed Big Mama. She would know what to do. I needed her to know about the monster that had emerged from hiding and attacked me. The Boogey Monster was real. He wasn't under my bed; he was in the bed with my mother. I needed her to make him go away. Although I knew she was only a phone call away, I was hesitant to speak with her. If I called her, she would have to tell my mother, who would tell the Boogey Monster. I clearly recalled his threat. He said he would kill us both if I told anyone. I knew there would be another day and another attempt on my body if I kept quiet. I would rather die than have him on top of me again. I would have to choose between an immediate death or assaults on my body that would eventually kill my spirit. I didn't want either death.

Everything around me changed overnight. Even the exhausted sofa, which doubled as the scene of the crime, changed its identity as well. Instead of being the spot where a family gathered to talk about the events of each day or huddled on to enjoy each other's company, it became the last place anyone would want to be. The only thing it needed to make its new identity official was crime scene tape. That sofa became the object of my disgust. It taunted me each time I entered and exited the room. It was unapologetically a constant reminder of that horrible, unforgettable night.

Life for me became a constant struggle after that night. I tried hard to put the entire episode out of my mind, but it was the only thing on my mind. I thought about it every day. I wondered how my mother didn't know that I was different. When I looked at her, how could she not notice that I was more woman than child? She never questioned the pain that was etched on my face and in my eyes. She never questioned how I reacted when he looked at me or when I was anywhere near him. Maybe she didn't love me like she said or she just didn't care. I didn't know. But I did know I couldn't count on her. She didn't wake up and save me.

The distasteful words he whispered in my ear became a broken record in my mind. According to his whispers, my mother and I were the walking dead. He knew he had the upper hand and he exploited his position. One day he told me that I wanted "it" to happen. He could tell by the way I looked at him. I couldn't believe he actually tried to justify his actions. But there was nothing that I did that led him to believe I welcomed his attack. I wanted to be invisible. I tried to hide any traces of femininity in my mother's baggy clothes. I never wanted to look cute anymore. I didn't need any attention. At night I slept in pajamas with blue jean shorts underneath to make it more difficult for another assault to occur. Maybe that would be enough to keep me safe. If all else failed, I would rely on the knife I buried in the sofa. I wouldn't be the only one who lost blood next time.

TEN

Confessions

It had been weeks since I felt like myself. I was sure the nausea I endured over several days was the result of the bug that was going around at school. All I wanted to do was sleep once the sick feeling passed. Even though I didn't want to go to school that day, for my own safety, I knew it was the best place for me. The nausea hit me again. I struggled to make it to the bathroom where I could relieve myself of my stomach's contents. Even after everything was gone, I continued to heave. The sweat beads on my forehead signified how hard my body was working to return to normal. The attempt to remain at school for the remainder of the day was futile. The nurse was forced to call my mother. They insisted on a trip to the doctor before they would allow me to return to school. We had no choice but to comply. As I waited in the doctor's office for our number to be called, the nausea finally ended. I was probably well enough to go back to school. But since we were already there, we stayed.

Finally, the diagnosis was made. The nurse wanted to talk to my mother alone. From beyond the limits of my sight, I heard screams of the word "no" in rapid succession. It sounded like a package of firecrackers was going off. Based on the reaction, I wondered how bad the news could have been for that poor person. I wondered what could have been that bad. When my mother approached, the expression on her face let me know all was not well. I realized it was my mother's voice that had exhibited such distress. She quickly grabbed my arm and rushed to exit the clinic. She pulled me behind her like a kite trying to take flight. I wondered what illness I contracted that warranted her reaction.

As we stood on the sidewalk, she turned me around and looked deeply into my eyes. She searched my soul for any signs that I had knowledge of my confirmed condition. She didn't find what she was looking for. Her expression softened. When she spoke, her voice was kind and soft when she shared my diagnosis. I never expected the word pregnant to bombard my ears. I wanted to throw up again. Big Mama told me how that could happen. I never thought it could happen to me. I didn't let some no good boy talk me into doing the "it" she had warned me about. That's what Big Mama said fast girls did. I was a good girl. I didn't even like boys like that. I finally understood how truly powerless I had been that night. Not only had some foreign object invaded my intimate space, it caused a byproduct of its presence to be caught up in my body. I was helpless and at the mercy of nature and consequences.

The shame and the guilt of my circumstances wouldn't allow me to hold my mother's gaze any longer. I dropped my head and focused on the cracks in the sidewalk. Before long, the tears fell in overlapping circles; first slowly, then as if someone turned on a sprinkler. The weight of the moment came down on me hard. My wobbly legs could no longer support me. I fell into my mother, grabbed ahold of her and sobbed. She gently rubbed my back and held my trembling body through the waves of tears.

Through her profession of love, she peppered the conversation with questions regarding the person responsible for my unexpected circumstance. I wanted to tell her, but the power of his words was stronger than my bravery. If I let those words escape into the universe, he would kill us both. That's what he said and I believed him. I couldn't afford to risk our lives. But since I was pregnant now, I had nothing to lose. The secret I tried to keep no longer existed. I couldn't go on like this and with the whole baby "thing", I knew I needed my mother's help. Through the tears and "I'm sorries", I whispered in her ear the name of my "Who".

Because I still couldn't look in her face, I was unaware of the wildness and anger that filled her eyes. She wrapped me tightly in her arms and hugged me like she wanted to make our bodies merge. She kept telling me that everything was going to be OK. No matter what anyone said, none of his actions were my fault. That's what I wanted to hear for a long time. Once I found my voice, I told my mother everything about that night and the continued gestures and stares directed at me. She held my hand and cried with me through my entire revelation.

My mother kissed me on my forehead and convinced me to go back to school. She had some business to take care of and didn't want me to go home alone. Letting go of her hand in front of the school was one of the hardest things I had ever done. Our fingers lingered until distance intervened. Had I known the significance of that last touch, I would have tried to hold on to her even longer.

ELEVEN

Payback

The flashing red and blue lights startled me as I turned the corner. The feeling of being safe was replaced with fear when I realized they were in front of my house. I recalled the threat he made to kill both of us if I ever told my mother about that night. I feared my mother was probably dead. I should have just kept my mouth shut. This was all my fault and now both of my parents were gone. Who would love me now? Not even Big Mama wanted me around. She sent me there and I ended up in the clutches of a monster. I prayed she would want me back in light of my current condition.

As I wormed my way through the crowd to get a closer view, I was swallowed up by the sea of strange faces and mumbling voices. Bits and pieces of a story came together from unfamiliar origins in the crowd.

The lady in the white sweater remarked, "A neighbor heard somebody screaming and hollering. She called the police."

The woman from apartment 2-D continued the conversation and commented, "The police found somebody tied to the bed. They had to cut 'em free."

The man in the blue hat joined in and added, "They took somebody out on a stretcher. The paramedics didn't think they would make it. No one could survive after all that blood loss."

The man with the beard was closest to the house and reported to the crowd, "Somebody still in there. I saw 'em sitting at the kitchen table smoking a cigarette and having a drink. For some reason, the police kept staring down at the sink shaking their heads. I don't know what they were looking for. Whatever it was, they were gonna have to cut that garbage disposal off to find it.

The older lady who lived next door shook her head and said, "Sure hope that child ain't in there. She could be hurt too".

I felt sick to my stomach after I heard what I concluded were the torturous last moments of my mother's life. I needed to get closer, but the pavement engulfed my feet and I assumed the role of curious onlooker. For my own sanity, I wanted to witness the capture of the monster that ruined my life and took my mother away from me. I wanted to defiantly look into his eyes, knowing he would never get the chance to make good on his promise to kill me too. I needed to be there to see him led away in handcuffs to a place where he wouldn't be able to hurt anybody else.

My vision of the front of the house was obscured when the police escorted the only witness to the earlier incident from the building. The shock of recognition from the crowd brought about an awkward silence after a collective gasp.

It didn't take long for the moans and gestures of surprise, mixed with the question "Why", to ripple through the crowd.

The hands of the offender were the first things that caught my attention. They were not as large as I remembered and were tinted in what reminded me of red finger paint. But it wasn't finger paint on those hands; it was blood. My eyes traveled upward to the face of the prisoner. I gasped as loudly as the crowd when I realized it was my mother in custody, not my tormentor. Looking back down her body I realized the hands were not the only place that held evidence of a violent attack. I screamed her name. Both she and the crowd searched for the source. Instinctively, I ran to her and wrapped my arms around her waist. I didn't care that the silver restraints didn't allow her to complete our embrace. My mother bent her head down and rested it on the top of my hair. I clung to her for as long as I could until the policeman pulled us apart. The front of her dress was the initial repository for my tears. They quickly found another place to congregate as they dripped down my cheek.

My mother's demeanor remained calm when our eyes connected. She told me about the letter on the kitchen table. She then told me to call Big Mama. Her eyes quickly scanned the crowd and saw compassion in the face of the next door neighbor lady. Before she was put into the car, she asked her to look after me until Big Mama could get there. I stood by the police car and begged the officer not to take my mother away. I knew my pleading was in vain. I was gently pulled away from the car before the door shut. My mother rested calmly into the back seat. I pressed my hand against the window in an unsuccessful attempt to experience one last touch. The next door neighbor lady pulled me away so the car could leave. My mother turned her head toward the back window and our eyes connected until space and distance prevailed. Even though she was not dead, we could no longer be together. I was without my mother. He still won. He took away my innocence and the presence of my mother in my life. It would be a long time before I saw my mother again.

The fifteen minutes we were given to collect some of my belongings were more than I wanted to spend inside that house of horrors. Now those walls could talk about two assaults that occurred within its bowels. I looked around the apartment and was overwhelmed by its current condition. I was mesmerized by the trail of blood that originated in the bedroom, traveled down the hallway, through the living room and ended abruptly at the kitchen sink. It clearly was not the way to Oz for the victim and the only red slippers were the blood-stained ones of my mother's. Someone in the crowd had mentioned the kitchen sink. The mystery surrounding its significance got the best of me. I started walking in the direction of the sink to get a closer look. My temporary guardian interrupted my mission. She reminded me of the letter on the table before she ushered me thru the front door. Once I reached the bottom of the steps, I turned around and looked back at the entrance. I realized the apartment now had what it needed for a long time…crime scene tape.

One of my greatest fears was that Big Mama wouldn't want me back, especially if she knew the difficult path I was about to undertake. Making that call to her was one of the hardest things I ever had to do. My emotions overtook my speech and I was unable to convey my need to be rescued. The next door neighbor lady intervened and explained everything. Big Mama instructed my caretaker not to allow me to go back to school, especially after the story about my mother made front page headlines and was the lead story on most local news outlets.

The story in the newspaper replaced the crowd's disjointed narration with their version of the facts. To the world, my mother caught her live-in lover in her house with another woman. She punished him for his betrayal in a manner that would have made Lorena Bobbitt proud. In a fit of rage, she tossed the offending appendage into the garbage disposal. It was still grinding its contents when the police arrived. As brutal as that all sounded, I had no pity for him. The punishment fit the crime.

Relief washed over me when the lock clicked on the bedroom door. I welcomed the sense of privacy and safety I hadn't enjoyed since I left Big Mama's house. Although I was in the house of a stranger, I found peace. There were no strange men in the house and I was able to sleep in a room with a door. After months of holding my breath, I was finally able to exhale.

I looked at the envelope from my mother for several minutes. I noticed splotches of blood and a red fingerprint on the back flap. It was minor compared to the amount of staining I witnessed on her garments. I took my finger and traced over my name in my mother's familiar handwriting. I wasn't ready to open the envelope yet. My mother had finally written me a letter. I thought about all the letters and packages that didn't come to Big Mama's house. Opportunities were missed to express words of joy and love I could have saved and revisited in my time of need.

After reading the letter from my mother in secret, I knew I had to keep it in a very safe place until I could share it with Big Mama. In her own words, my mother explained the rationale behind her retribution differently than the accounts reported in the news. The letter was brief, but powerful. Through her words I saw the emotion she held back during our last embrace.

I don't have much time left before the police come and there are things I really need to say. Baby I love you and I am asking you to forgive me. I messed up your life because I couldn't get mine together. I kept trying to find your daddy again, but I couldn't. So, I settled for someone I knew was not good for me. I don't want you to think any of this is your fault, it's mine. I didn't protect you enough. I told him before you came that if he ever touched you, I'd kill him. I hope I did. He will never be able hurt another innocent child like he hurt you. Go with your Big Mama. She is the only one I can trust with your heart. She will always protect you and love you unconditionally. I am going away for a long time, but it was all worth it because I know you are safe now. Please never forget how much I love you.

I had often wondered if my mother had loved me, but I now had confirmation of the depth of her love for me. Her apparent lack of concern for the dysfunction under her roof was not as I imagined. She had made the consequences of his betrayal obvious before my arrival. She had attempted to follow through with her promise once the violation of the established ground rules became evident. On the one hand I was elated. He received what he deserved. But on the other hand, I too was punished again for his actions. His destructive influence continued to spread its shadows over my life.

The familiar face of my grandmother filled my heart with joy. I ran into the safety of her waiting arms. Our embrace lasted for a long time. She allowed me to absorb all the love I needed from her. I hadn't realized how much I missed her kind, loving face until that moment. Big Mama visited my mother at the jail before she came to pick me up. She was informed of his true crime, her punishment and the far-reaching consequences of his actions. The impact on my immediate future and my life as a whole were unknowns. The look in her eyes let me know she was prepared for the daunting task that awaited us both.

While we gathered my belongings, Big Mama asked about the letter from my mother. I raised the pant leg of my jeans and retrieved it from my sock. After the letter was read, she immediately tore it up into little pieces and put them in her purse. Other than the two of us, no one else could bear witness to the content of the confession. Although I understood Big Mama's actions, I realized the documented evidence of love from my mother was confetti. All of my mother was gone from my life for the foreseeable future. I was left with memories and dreams that would gradually fade as my life moved forward.

TWELVE

Back at Big Mama's House

When I returned to Big Mama's house, I had no age identity. I was no longer a child, but not yet a woman. My mind and body didn't agree. I struggled to find myself somewhere in between who I wanted to be and who my body forced me to become. Even though she told me she was thankful I was there, Big Mama treated me differently. She looked at me, but it appeared she never actually saw me. She desperately wanted to see the child she sent away whole and full of joy. The spirit of that child vanished when I left the Greyhound bus station. What returned was a fragmented, soiled woman/child. Other times she looked at me and fought a losing battle with the tears that found their way to freedom and escaped down her cheek. I wasn't sure if she was crying about me or for me.

The first few days back were hard for me. I was a bundle of emotions. My mind never calmed down long enough for the magic of sleep to bring peace and comfort to my troubled soul. I felt so ashamed of my current condition. I feared Big Mama thought less of me for losing the change in my pocketbook. After all the conversations we'd had about that precious commodity, I couldn't hold on to it. How would she be able to look at me the same when there was undisputed evidence of the virginal betrayal that had undoubtedly occurred? I wanted to remain in solitary confinement in my room so no one would be constantly reminded of a consequence that resulted in such pain and tears for all of us. Big Mama gave me my space for a few days, but decided it was time to confront the problem head-on. We needed to clear the air between us.

The creaky floors that concealed my presence during my snooping expeditions were not so kind to Big Mama as she made her way to my room. Without speaking, she sat on the bed, pulled me into her bosom and gently rocked me. "He hurt me big Mama" was all I could get out before I began to cry uncontrollably. I babbled unrecognizable syllables that only I could decipher as I tried to tell my story. I wanted so much for her to know that I was a good girl and that I didn't want any of this to happen.

Big Mama continued to hold me and softly said, "I know baby. Your mother told me everything. I know he raped you."

Hearing those words helped me gain control of my emotions. Those words acquitted me from feeling like I had contributed to the actions of that rapist. Finally the tears stopped and my breathing returned to normal as it transitioned from hiccup-like spasms to deep cleansing breaths. After I calmed down enough to continue our conversation, Big Mama once again began to help me truly understand the depths of the assault that occurred on both my mind and my body.

"It was an ugly violent crime over which you were powerless. You were an innocent child. He forced you into a womanly situation long before your mind and body were ready. None of this was your fault. I understand the actions your mother took. She wanted to protect you from the courts so she told them he was caught cheating in her own house. The police called it a crime of passion and indeed it was. It was her passion for you that caused her to take the law into her own hands. Thank God your Big Daddy didn't get to him. When he learned what happened to you, the first words out of his mouth were, "Is he dead?" When he learned what your mother did he said, "That's even better...Saved me a bullet." Her actions had cost her dearly, but maybe you will be able to understand the depths of a mother's love in the very near future. Pretty soon we have to decide what to do about this baby you are carrying. You are gonna have to decide if you want to keep it or put it up for adoption."

A blank stare greeted Big Mama. I didn't know what to say. I didn't want to think about any of it. I just wanted my mother.

THIRTEEN

A Defining Moment

The room was again quiet and still after Big Mama tucked me in bed and insisted I get some rest. I closed my eyes, but my mind continued to replay our conversation. RAPE. That was the word Big Mama used to describe what happened to me. It was such an ugly word with an uglier meaning that justly identified the act. For such a small word, it was very powerful. The dictionary had its definition, but I had my own. It couldn't be summed up as one singular event. It was continual and represented more than the physical act. It took years for me to truly understand the power of that four letter word. I found that it will haunt you, challenge you, taunt you, ridicule you, dismantle you, shame you, and in my case, impregnate you. It will hold you captive until you become strong enough to break free. Both my physical and mental musculature was too underdeveloped for something of that magnitude.

The frame this crime crafted surrounded many portraits of unwilling subjects, seeking to define their existence and to occupy a place of prominence in their lives. Its victim's gallery constantly had showings of new members of all shapes, sizes, colors, ages and descriptions. It didn't discriminate or pacify and gleefully welcomed all patrons. If one portrait dropped out of the frame, another new one took its place. Some portraits had been there for decades and showed signs of feathering as life took its toll on those who couldn't break free. Others turned to liquid or powdered courage to survive. They would never be content until their showing ended and they were finally at eternal peace.

I didn't want the rape to define me. I didn't want to feel victimized forever. I wanted my portrait removed from that frame. This wrong would not be easy to right and I didn't know where to start. I wasn't big enough or strong enough to confront my abuser. I had plenty of rage and anger to fuel my battle for freedom, but I didn't know how to channel it. My mother released some of her anger and sought retribution by mutilation, but I wasn't convinced she considered how my life would be without her. Being raped wasn't supposed to have happened to me or anyone for that matter. I didn't realize how long it would take to claim victory over that one defining moment.

FOURTEEN

Baby Mama Drama

C onflict raged inside me regarding the passive intruder and never allowed me to have any peace. I didn't feel like an expectant mother, but more like a baby dispenser. I did not like this "thing" and I knew I could never love "it". How could I bond with or love something that was sourced from evil. It represented all the things I had lost in my life. I didn't want to be constantly reminded of those unwanted changes.

My vision would always be distorted if I looked into its face. It would be watermarked with the letter "R." Without a doubt, I knew its features would remind me of the biological person who donated to its unwanted existence. If I chose to love it, those actions would represent disloyalty to my mother and everything she sacrificed for me. But wasn't this her fault as well as his? Deep down, she knew something about that man was not right; she threatened him before I arrived. I blamed her for not protecting me. If I wasn't important enough for her to choose me, and she really loved me, this "thing" would never have a chance. I didn't want or need it. Without a doubt, I didn't think I could ever love it.

My body continued to change as it accepted nature's version of the truth. I could no longer conceal from my reality certain thoughts and feelings. My tender breasts ripened even more and roundness continued to fill out places in my face and hips. I had convinced myself that without proof of life, the whole "with-child" status was not real; it was just a theory. I was not sure if I really believed it, but I clung to that thought as a survival technique. The longer I could put off this reality, the better. I needed to protect my sanity. But like a cruel puppet master, fate decided to prove who was in charge.

The sensation of life's proof was like nothing I ever felt before. The faint flutter inside my core felt as if I had swallowed a butterfly whose wings rapidly flapped against my insides trying to find space to fly again. To my surprise, I giggled in amazement at the thrill and recognition that another human was actually attached to my insides. Someone was totally dependent on me for survival. Neither I nor my body could ignore this miracle. All the changes to my body contradicted the desires of my heart. I had no choice but to wait and accept what nature had in store for me.

FIFTEEN

Freedom

My sleep was interrupted by twinges of pain similar to those that accompanied my monthly visitor. Because I had no reference point, I thought it was just part of being pregnant. The intensity of the pain increased and became more frequent. My mind searched for explanations for this foreign sensation.

I tried desperately to find a spot in the bed that would somehow make the pain less noticeable. Those attempts were futile. The ripples of pain in my back and abdomen caused my body to go into the fetal position. I screamed at the top of my lungs for Big Mama while I protectively clutched my protruding abdomen.

I felt an uncontrollable urge to push that could not be denied. After doing so, I felt my secret seeping out of me as the warmth of its lifeline spread beneath the spot where I lay. The creaky floors of the hallway emphasized the quickness of her response to my anguish. It was all over before Big Mama could respond to my cries for help. She found me laying there confused and conflicted about the spontaneity of this new truth. As unceremoniously as this life started, it ended in the same abrupt manner; without warning and without taking my feelings into consideration.

I knew what I felt in my body, but I did not want to acknowledge with my eyes the aftermath of the natural selection process. Big Mama helped me remove my soiled garments. Everything was wrapped up in the sheets before she helped me make my way to the bathroom to get cleaned up. I was glad to leave that room. If I never looked back at the last remains of "it", I could leave all of this behind me. Maybe all my sorrows would be wrapped up and tossed away in that sheet as easily as it had been to replace one sheet with another. By tomorrow it would be a bygone memory and I could start my life over again. I could reset my life and push "play" at the happy place it had been before I left the safety of Big Mama's house and went to live with my mother. I was not sure that would happen, but I was willing to try.

Big Mama put it best when she said it was just the Lord having His way. I was confused by my reaction. Although I said I wanted no part of "it", turmoil brewed inside. I wondered how it would have felt to be a mother. I knew what kind of mother mine had been while my father was alive. Hurt and sadness took over and transformed her into someone I didn't recognize. The most powerful role model in my life abandoned me.

I knew what I thought would have been the embodiment of a great mother. At first I was sure I could have lived up to that standard. The flaws in my theory surfaced the more the pregnancy advanced. The first time I perceived any features to be those of its father's, I was not sure my actions would have been appropriate for a loving mother. That would have required an inner strength I had not yet developed. But still, I continued to get stuck on the "what ifs". What if it was a boy; would it know how to love or would it become a predator, just like its father? What if people asked questions about its paternity and I had no plausible explanation? What if I gave "it" away, would it somehow find me? What if I was unable to let go once I saw its face? What if my father was still alive?

SIXTEEN

Funeral Procession

No one in town knew about my pregnancy and Big Mama intended to keep it that way. Small towns had few secrets and this was one that never needed to see the light of day. There would be too many questions from too many strangers. The last thing we wanted was any correlation between my condition and the infamous actions of my mother. A doctor's visit was never an option. Instead, Big Mama called her midwife friend who verified what we already knew was true; I was no longer an expectant mother. I was physically free, but still emotionally bound.

Being the woman she was, Big Mama's morals dictated we give the unborn child a proper burial. She insisted that all life was sacred and throwing away the baby like a piece of garbage was an insult to our maker. Both I and the baby were innocent victims in this tragedy. Neither of us needed to be punished further for our existence or these circumstances.

I dreaded our appointment with destiny. I didn't want to participate in the reverent sham. I didn't understand how they could honor the memory of something whose life had no value and represented such pain and suffering for me.

No one asked me if I even wanted to be there. But no one ever asked me anything; not my mother, not that man and certainly not this "thing" that continued to make a mockery of my existence.

My life had been ruined and I was forced to celebrate the object of the discord in my life. I felt my family betrayed me and overlooked how I would be impacted. Since I had no other option, I would dutifully stand there, but I would refuse to speak or feel anything. I wasn't supposed to care. I now had my freedom. I was burying a painful part of my past and that was exactly what I thought I needed.

We went deep in the woods on the back part of the property to find an appropriate gravesite for "it". At the base of a random tree, we stopped and prepared the earth to receive its homecoming gift. The cross that was carved on the tree would be the only outward source of recognition that life would ever have. It could never be spoken of or celebrated beyond that moment. I hoped the makeshift ceremony would exorcise some of the demons that lingered inside me. I was anxious for everything to be over. Surely the finality of these actions would mark the start of the carefree teenage years every girl should enjoy before the heaviness of adulthood caused them to buckle under the pressure.

When the first bit of dirt settled on the shoe box, it felt like a ton of bricks settled on my chest. My mind flashed back to the day ceremonial dirt was placed on my daddy's casket. I remembered the sadness in everyone's eyes. In contrast, I was faced with a loss about which I wouldn't allow myself to feel anything. Although I witnessed the next shovel full of dirt go down into the hole, it felt as if the dirt covered my face. Suddenly, I couldn't breathe. Sadness embraced me like the hug of an old friend. I gave in to the awkwardness of an unexpected avenue of relief. I closed my eyes and let it comfort me for as long as it wanted. Joy and grief competed for my mind. It was hard to tell which one had the upper hand. The screaming I thought was only in my head actually came from my mouth. The shrillness and the volume interrupted the burial ceremony. Anxiety and panic gripped my body and my eyes wildly searched for an exit strategy. My legs started moving. I didn't realize I was running until I stumbled and fell on debris along the path. Pain radiated from my scraped knees and hands. I quickly got up and willed myself forward. My ultimate goal was to get as far away from that tree as possible.

When I stopped running, the trail of tears didn't. I made my way onto the porch swing, rested my head against its back and tried to catch my breath. Big Mama found me sitting there staring into space, looking at nothing in particular. She didn't say a word; she just sat down, held my hand and stared too. Before long, we both were soothed by the rhythmic sounds of the creaky swing that had been our special place during my youthful days. Slowly I made my way into the safety of Big Mama's arms where she hummed songs that spoke to me even though there were no words. Peace found its way to my fourteen year old mind. I was finally able to take a deep breath. That night, I slept like the baby I was. I was home, safe and free; just as I had been 143 days ago.

When I returned to Big Mama's house I felt like the China doll that had been taken out of its protective box, played with unmercifully until broken, then cast aside. Since I had been freed of those unwanted obligations, I wanted a new beginning. One Sunday afternoon, Big Daddy came out and sat beside me on the porch swing. He was not as vocal as Big Mama, so when he spoke, I knew it was important that I listened. He put his arms around me and said, "One of our biggest regrets is that we sent you back to your mother. If we had known she was living with a man, we never would have let you out of our sight." I saw the pain on his face as he struggled to convey the right words. "No child should ever have to experience the awful things you have gone through. But, if you keep moving forward, the past will always be behind you. Don't make it more important in your life than it is."

He looked off into the distance and said, "You are such a special child. You remind me so much of your father. You're a fighter, just like he was, and smart as a whip. You got that from him too."

I smiled in admiration about the comparison to my father. I was honored by the compliment.

Big Daddy took his index finger and softly tapped my temple. Then he told me, "Knowledge is power. If you get it in your head, no one can take it away from you. All the rest of the nonsense can wait."

I hugged him hard then curled up closer to him to receive all the love and support that emanated from his being. I hadn't heard positive affirmation from a male in such a long time. To have it come from him meant more than he knew. I really missed my daddy, but was grateful Big Daddy was there for me.

SEVENTEEN

Why Me?

A fter all the events of the last few months, I was happy when school started again. I was ready to keep the past behind me and move toward the future. I needed to reconnect with people my own age. I was forced to be isolated and alone when I was "with child". After being hidden from the world, I needed to be set free. I observed old friends from my younger days and was anxious to model their innocent ways.

For the next three years or so, I was content with the mundane existence that went along with high school life. I was a good student and welcomed the distraction I found in textbooks and regimented schedules. It made me feel as close to a normal teenager as possible. The distance grew wider between old heartaches and the hope for my future. But try as I might, I never could shed the restrictive cocoon of fear that constantly surrounded me. I feared someone would figure out the secrets of my past and my lies would be exposed to the world. I found it easy to welcome exchanges from the girls, but was terrified by any boy who looked at me too long. I didn't want that kind of attention. I tried to hide myself from the world. I wore baggy clothes and avoided any male contact. Any lingering glances brought back memories of other unwanted stares. I cowered under the perceived inappropriate advance. I knew what could happen if I looked too good. My only goal was to survive. I was sure my actions were as attractive as insect repellent to mosquitos and as juvenile as a fifth grader. But I didn't care. All I cared about was moving from day to day without incident.

I never wondered if anyone ever paid attention to me in school. I didn't care. I was content to just exist until graduation. The hallways were crowded noisy passageways filled with laughter and fun emitting from groups I was not a part of. I aspired to remain invisible in my own skin. By doing so, I disqualified myself from normal high school frivolity before I ever gave it a chance to welcome me. I felt my sordid past made me and my emotional frailty unattractive to kids my own age. I felt unworthy of the lightness that accompanied my age group. The shackles of my past still surrounded me. They made clanking sounds each time I thought about moving forward. They subtly reminded me that I was not totally free. I longed for something good to come along and distract the past long enough for me to put some distance between it and my future. But each day mocked those longings as it delivered the same non-eventful offerings as the day before. Maybe tomorrow became my repetitive thought. Even though parts of me declared that mindset useless, a granule of hope believed the odds would shift in my favor one day.

Every day had been the same until that one. I saw him

staring at something in my direction, but never thought he was looking at me. I thought his attention was fixed on someone more interesting than me. I never thought anyone would want to look at me. I believed my aura lacked confidence and approachability. As he moved in my direction, I turned my attention to the contents of my locker. To my disbelief, he stopped right in front of me. "Hi, my name is Adam. What's yours?" I was frozen in my thoughts and looked at him in stunned silence. A crackly sound escaped from somewhere inside my throat. I managed to say, "Eva."

The corny joke he told made me laugh. It served as the bridge to further conversation. I enjoyed our brief exchange and recounted the punchline of that joke throughout the day. Each time I thought about Adam, I smiled at his corniness and the simplicity of our encounter. Underneath the camouflage I used for self-preservation, he saw something in me I thought I lost. He saw the real me and I enjoyed being looked at as a person, not as prey. It made me feel human again; like the carefree teenager I longed to be. I had forgotten how nice it was to have a male friend. At that time, a friend was all I was able to handle.

It didn't take long for me to become more comfortable with my new friend. Adam continued to make time for me and I looked forward to his presence. I saw changes in both my attitude and appearance as portions of the fear cocoon fell away. I often lingered in the hallway longer than necessary, trying to spot him in the crowd. The more time we spent together, the less tarnished I felt. I wasn't sure how long our connection would last, but I was encouraged and delighted each day it continued.

I didn't know how to categorize our relationship, but I liked it for what it was. I had developed a friendship with someone from the opposite sex and I was not afraid. It appeared the dating ritual started before I had a chance to reject it. Did I actually have a boyfriend? I decided to mentally disavow the boyfriend theory and keep him in the "friend" category. One thing for sure, Big Mama wouldn't be happy about whatever I called it. She would have no qualms about making her feelings known.

I knew beyond any reasonable doubt there was no way Big Mama would agree to any boy courting me at this juncture of my life. Our friendship had to be one that was for school days only. But Adam was persistent. He frequently asked about coming to my house. When I couldn't object any longer, I agreed he could come one Saturday afternoon. Maybe if he stopped by on a day when both my grandparents were home, it would be better than if he came when it was just Big Mama. She would eat him alive. She would come at him with a litany of questions that rivaled the ones on Jeopardy. I hoped that when he was brave enough to visit, he had a strong stomach, good deodorant and stainless steel underwear.

EIGHTEEN

Meet the Parents

When I woke up that Saturday morning, I had no idea my suitor would pay me a visit that day. I thought all the roadblocks I threw up would have made that day non-viable for a long time, if ever. When I heard a car pull up into the gravel driveway, I abandoned my morning chores and immediately went out onto the front porch. I stood there in utter disbelief when Adam got out of the vehicle. I felt like the princess whose knight in four-wheeled armor had come to rescue her from the monotony of a mundane weekend existence. I suppressed a gleeful squeal when he saw me and flashed a beautiful smile in my direction. Our eyes locked. We remained entranced for what seemed an eternity. I wanted to linger in that moment and experience the same freedom we shared during school hours.

We were in our own world. Big Mama brought me back to reality when she asked, "Who is that?" When I told her he was one of my friends from school, she gave me a look that would have severely wounded me had it been a knife. Big Mama stood there with her hands on her hips and looked back and forth between us. As if she read my thoughts, she slowly and sternly admonished me for any thoughts of going out to greet my visitor. Through gritted teeth she grunted, "Don't you run your butt out to that car. Any boy that is worth your time comes into the house and respectfully acknowledges your parents and you as a young lady. You better not move off this porch! Now go sit down." Her long index finger, that rivaled that of any self-respecting witch, was pointed directly at me. She motioned for me to move in the direction of the porch swing. I complied.

I had no choice but to show the porch swing my annoyance with her directives. It showed no mercy on my backside after I plopped down on it a little too hard. If I didn't know better, I would have sworn the creaky sounds coming from the swing were its form of laughter at my expense. But I continued to assume my defiant posture with my bottom lip poked out and my arms crossed. The entire time I thought, "I hope he didn't hear what Big Mama said; that was embarrassing!"

Big Daddy heard all the commotion and joined Big Mama in the examination of the stranger. I strained my neck and ears and tried to intercept portions of the hushed words and glances exchanged between the two of them. For reasons unknown to me, Big Daddy went back into the house. I stood up briefly and peered anxiously through the door. Panic set in when he opened the gun case. My wobbly knees buckled under the weighty circumstances and I lost my balance. I stumbled backward and the swing caught me before I fell butt first on the wooden planks of the porch. More creaky laughter from the swing filled the air.

Once Adam made it to the porch, he noticed my demeanor and seemed to have a "what the hell is going on" look on his face. He looked as if he wanted to turn and run back to his car. If I were any kind of friend, I would have encouraged him to leave before Big Daddy came back outside. I wanted to warn my friend about the rifle, but I couldn't. It felt like I had glue in my mouth and the words were held hostage because of a lack of saliva.

There was an awkward silence as he stood on the front porch in front of Big Mama. He cleared his throat, spoke to me and introduced himself to Big Mama. She politely acknowledged his presence, but kept looking nervously back over her shoulders in the direction of the front door. His bowel control was tested when Big Daddy re-emerged from the house, sat down beside me and started to polish his rifle. His eyes continually looked in Adam's direction.

Once he got settled on the swing he asked, "Who are you and what are your intentions with my granddaughter?" He never took his eyes off Adam as we rocked back and forth on the swing. Beads of sweat appeared on his forehead and raced each other down his face, to the collar of his t-shirt. With wide eyes and a sticky throat, my friend managed to nervously disclose his lineage. Big Daddy pondered those facts then proclaimed that he knew his family. What he didn't say then was, "And they ain't worth two dead flies", a statement he later communicated to Big Mama when he thought I was not around.

Big Daddy probably knew there was no acceptable response to his rhetorical question regarding Adam's intentions. I felt he was toying with Adam and his emotions. He made us both suffer through his interrogation. He was unable to answer the riddle and stood paralyzed in his thoughts and actions trying to figure out what to do next. There was no hole in the front porch I could crawl into, so I sat on the swing and braced myself for the worst. I thought I should close my eyes so I could honestly say I didn't witness any of the impending violence, but my eyes would not look away. They darted wildly between my friend and my grandfather. I wanted to chronicle every portion of the potential horror movie. I internally scolded myself about my decision to relent to his visitation request. I should have just told him to stay away.

All I wanted was for my grandparents to give Adam a chance. I wanted them to see the person I became acquainted with. Something about me changed after I met im. Just last week, Big Mama commented on how she saw glimpses of the old me. Genuine smiles returned to my eyes and joy radiated from my being. My grandparents were very overprotective, and I understood why. When I first returned to their home, Big Mama expressed guilt about her perceived role in my exposure to that predator. We both knew his actions had nothing to do with either of us. That man was broken at his core long ago. We were just casualties of his unresolved anger. But Adam was not that man; he was someone my own age that had the courage to meet them face-to-face.

After he looked him up and down several times, Big

Daddy put down his rifle and motioned for Adam to take a walk with him. Since the rifle no longer posed an immediate threat, I was convinced he would jump off the porch and run to his car. He accepted my grandfather's invitation. He was either brave or foolish. I hoped he told someone where to start the search in case he didn't make it back home that day. As long as they didn't go into the woods, he would be safe. Those woods held secret graves. No one would know if one more body was there. Big Daddy often used a pistol to shoot snakes that wandered out from hiding and got too close to the house. I wasn't sure if Adam was excluded from that category in his eyes. I prayed he would leave our property in one piece.

They wandered around the back of the property, deeply engrossed in what appeared to be a one-sided discussion led by the elder. Adam mostly wrung his hands and nodded in affirmation as he endured the conversation. Once I thought I saw him flash a smile, but it might have just been a grimace or maybe even gas. Relief washed over my face when the interrogation concluded and they finally returned to the front of the house. To my surprise, Big Daddy looked Adam in the eyes and shook his hand. Then, he gathered his newly polished metal and wood truth serum and went back into the house. I wasn't the only one caught off guard by that exchange. Big Mama's jaw dropped and her eyes bulged half-way out of their sockets. She quickly followed Big Daddy back into the house, determined to get the details about their man-talk.

Both Adam and I let out an audible sigh of relief when he sat down beside me on the swing. After the mental warfare we both experienced, we were exhausted and thankful for the porch swing. I was proud of Adam. He had endured the parental gauntlet unscathed. No soiling was evident, visually or aromatically, on his jeans, but beads of sweat found their way to the collar of his dark colored t-shirt. It looked like a fabric necklace. But I didn't care about any of that. My prince had rescued me. For his bravery, he earned the right to spend time with me.

We allowed ourselves to relax and enjoyed each other's company. The gentle breeze cooled us down and soothed our frazzled nerves. Playful banter and genuine joy radiated from us for hours. After he drove away, I remained on the swing and replayed the events of that day. What started out as a day from hell, ended up as a small slice of heaven. I knew it was one Saturday I would not soon forget.

NINETEEN

Tongue Tied

I enjoyed the purity of our relationship. Adam definitely captured my heart. I was so comfortable around him. I never tired of his companionship. The more things I discovered about Adam, the more I rediscovered parts of myself that were dormant and unreachable for many years. I remembered who I was before adult problems flip-flopped with my carefree years. I didn't recognize who I was forced to become. Although my family did their best to make me believe I was still the same person before I was raped, I couldn't accept their version of facts. It wasn't fully rooted in honesty. Their version was skewed by familial love. I appreciated their efforts, but it was Adam who helped me reclaim my childhood.

Big Mama allowed regular visits from Adam, but she didn't make it easy for us. Either we followed her rules or the visits would be discontinued. Before he was allowed to come into the house, Big Mama laid out a conduct list that clearly came from the "Hell No" book of unsuccessful relationships, page 666. We hated her overbearing, restrictive rules, but we tolerated them. It was the only way to spend time together away from school.

During my youth, my friends and I captured grasshoppers and put them in jars filled with grass. Someone told us they made tobacco from the grass they chewed. Probing eyes constantly stared into those jars from every angle. No one wanted to miss the big event. Big Mama's constant peering through windows and screen doors made us feel like those grasshoppers. I realized I owed those innocent creatures an apology for the cruelty of our actions.

There were times when Adam visited that he came no further than the front porch. On one of those nights the moonlight was bright enough to cast shadows and the stars brightly populated the sky. I couldn't think of a place I wanted to be more. We had been playfully laughing and hitting each other for most of his visit. Out of the blue, he grabbed my arms, pulled me close and kissed me. I wasn't prepared for the intimacy of a kiss. My body and my senses went into overdrive the second our lips connected. In my mind, the world stopped. All I could concentrate on was the physical portion of such a spiritual act. After our lips parted and my eyes opened again, the firework show going on in my mind relocated to my body. I marveled at how tingly and giddy I felt. The descriptions in the romance novels were nowhere close to the range of emotions that surfaced during such a brief encounter. The weakness in my knees would have caused me to fall had Adam's arms not been around me. I leaned deeper into his arms. He held me tighter. I felt comfortable in his arms. I had no objection to the second kiss I received before we said goodnight.

I must have floated into the house because I didn't recall walking up the stairs to my bedroom. I sat on my bed, closed my eyes and relived my first kiss. I was tingly all over again. I fell backward onto the bed with both hands over my heart. It was still racing. All of these feelings were so new for me. I realized how odd it was that I had been an expectant mother, but had never been romantically kissed. I witnessed my mother and father kiss and giggle when they embraced. I remembered how they looked into each other's eyes. My first kiss gave me a glimpse into the connection they shared. After we kissed, I started to understand more about the components of a normal male-female relationship.

TWENTY

Choices

The deeper our romance developed, the more passionate our kisses became. When new sensations centered in specific regions, Big Mama's omen about boys and my body flooded my mind. There were times when my body reacted unexpectedly to his touch and I disengaged from his embrace to regain my balance. Adam pushed things to the limit, but understood when his advances reached the boundaries of my comfort zone. Although his hands stopped, his words didn't. He told me the bodily awakenings I experienced were normal and there should be no shame or judgement about what I felt. He wanted us to express our feelings in other ways that would give us a deeper connection. If he was referring to becoming acquainted with my pocketbook change, I wasn't quite sure how I felt about that.

After what I experienced from my mother's boyfriend, I had no intention of connecting with anybody like that ever again. But based on our physical and verbal connection, that was the path Adam wanted to travel. He had no clue about my past. He probably made assumptions about my experience level, based on my comfort level with my new feelings and desires. There was no way I could tell him about my traumatic past experience. It would overshadow any chance of the normal future our bodies could enjoy. Since I couldn't be totally honest with him, I wondered if I was being unfair. It would be unfair to punish Adam for a crime he didn't commit, if our physical union could produce something magical and renewing. I wondered if an intimate physical connection would clear away some emotional baggage by replacing brutality and resentment with softness and love. I rationalized that I could possibly find a physical resolution to a physical injustice. In the midst of all those thoughts, Big Mama's conversation about slick-talking boys and their intentions rumbled through my head. I was confused by thoughts and emotions over which I had limited control. One thing I did have control over was my own body. All decisions about it would be mine. I had promised that to myself a long time ago. I had no intention of voiding that commitment.

My mind was torn by the constant bombardment of conflicting messages from Adam and Big Mama. My own personal thoughts were secondary. No matter who I listened to, I would lose. If I followed Big Mama's directives, she won. If I followed Adam's wishes, he won. We couldn't all win. We each wanted different things for different reasons. I had to choose what was best for me. Since I couldn't trust my own mind, I decided to follow my heart.

He slowly moved my emotions toward emancipation and I kept following his lead. I was two different people; one person at home and another when I was around Adam.

If Big Mama knew of the inappropriate, but liberating touching that went on between us, she would question the deviation from my home training. No doubt she would forbid further contact with him. But clearly she was too old to understand how much joy Adam brought to my life. I knew I was loved by my father and Big Daddy, but what I experienced with Adam was different. I knew that I loved him and he often professed his love for me. That was what mattered most. The rest would have to work itself out based on our love.

One of Big Mama's cardinal rules was that Adam couldn't be in the house while they weren't at home. It was not by accident that we broke her rule. It was time to prove my love for Adam. One week prior, Big Mama had the "talk" with me again. Maybe she sensed our intentions and wanted to fortify my resolve. She reiterated the need to guard the change in my pocketbook from interloping males who looked to conquer the next naive female. I knew she meant well, but I was old enough to make my own decisions about my body. The first time my intimate space was entered, it was on someone else's terms. This time it would be my decision.

TWENTY-ONE

My Change

It started with a gentle kiss and moved rapidly toward a more forceful and passionate tenure. Adam looked deeply into my eyes and professed his love for me. Unbridled desire coursed through our bodies after we removed our garments and liberated our bodies. Without shame, we willingly exposed our exterior and interior beings. We marveled at each other's temple. It was nothing like the intruding eyes of my attacker who relied on opportunity and cracks in doors to catch glimpses of my exposed body. He breathlessly whispered in my ear how beautiful I was as he began to lead me further into our love journey. I committed myself fully to the long-awaited natural rite of passage to womanhood.

The gentleness of his touch was feathery and soothing. He caressed my body and planted quick kisses on my face and neck. Although immersed in the moment, pieces of my mind traveled back to my only other encounter with the opposite sex. When the brutal memories tried to encroach on my happiness, I shunned those thoughts. It was a different experience, even though biologically the same. The bonds we formed during our courtship made the closeness of our bodies seem so natural. Innocence bred bravery and I explored places on his body that responded to my touch. Passionate kisses and caresses drew me further into inevitability. He stroked my breasts before he suckled them like a newborn babe looking for milk. My mind couldn't keep up with the pace of desire. Each new feeling longed to be remembered, but I couldn't think, I could only feel and absorb.

Taking directions from our bodies, he moved on me with measured pressure that served as the gateway to unexpected plateaus. I matched his rhythm to receive a deeper connection that occurred as naturally as breathing. All I could focus on was the anticipation of the next movement and the newness of carnal desires meant to be sacredly shared in marriage. A myriad of emotional, sensual and physical sensations collided. They culminated in involuntary spasms of release that couldn't be contained within the limits of my body. I savored the sensations that no longer were confined within me. Waves of contentment cascaded through my body and fell off the tips of my appendages. Only tiny mists of perspiration and exhaustion remained. I realized I was no longer a virgin.

I cuddled with Adam, content with my decision to unite our bodies. Our love union felt different than I could have ever imagined. It was soft, intimate and beautiful. I was in awe of the powerful electricity that could be generated by two willing bodies. Ironically, in the same bed where a life drained from me, a cauldron of pleasure was revealed to me. I wondered why Big Mama left out the pleasure details during our "talks".

What a night it had been. I began to understand the complexity of the human body and how perception can be altered by circumstances. If those feelings were the ultimate objective of intimate human companionship, I understood how sound reasoning became fickle when the union of the heart and body were joined by passion. I gained insight into, but did not condone, the actions of my offender. After that night, I knew there would be a need for water hoses in my future.

Being with a man was intoxicating. Once the joys of fleshly desires were unlocked, I wanted more. Our first time was so beautiful. I wanted the opportunity to recapture the magical tension of that first encounter. It was illogical to deny myself the hidden pleasures I discovered that were far more valuable than the leprechaun's rainbow treasure. I considered myself a woman with yearnings that could only be quenched by the love of Adam.

I had grown folks' business of my own to conceal and I definitely knew how to keep a secret. We became reckless and deceitful after our initial encounter. I lied to my grandparents, skipped school and violated any location and space available for our secret sessions. I better understood some of my mother's choices about the importance of male companionship. I was Adam's woman. Our love grew stronger each time we added to the depth of our commitment. Nothing meant more to me than the love we shared. Nothing, not even the hostile tactics of Big Mama, could tear us apart.

TWENTY-TWO

Bundle Up

The smell of Big Mama's breakfast wafted up the stairs to my nostrils. Usually I welcomed the aroma and quickly made my way downstairs for breakfast. That day, I scampered to the bathroom before the contents of my stomach exposed themselves. I opted to take extra time in the bathroom and limited my food consumption to dry toast. The intermittent uncooperative nature of my stomach continued for weeks. Big Mama noticed it. I was concerned by the quizzical stares and her overall body language toward me. One morning she asked, "Is there something you need to tell me?" My mouth said no, but my mind was not sure.

During the ride to school, I experienced a light bulb moment. The word pregnant popped into my mind. I couldn't believe it hadn't been the first diagnosis of my internal rebellion. I had been with child previously, but nothing about that situation was normal. I didn't want to remember anything about that agonizing event. I tried to bury every aspect of that time in the woods behind our house. I understood the anatomy of reproduction and our bodies connected enough to have required several sessions with the water hose. If my suspicions were correct, the trajectory of my life would shift drastically.

We met at my locker between second and third period. Our normal embrace was supplemented by my whispered suspicions. He reacted as if he had come in contact with a hot surface. The nervous chuckle demonstrated the unexpected nature of my news. He fought hard to keep his composure. As we walked to my classroom, we agreed to suspend our conversation until later. At lunch, we talked about how many times we had spent my pocketbook change and the last time Mother Nature visited me. The preliminary calculations did not add up in our favor. The suspense was over when the drugstore test gave me a passing fertility grade. We were speechless. The consequences of our actions were staring us right in the face. Neither one of us was prepared for that diagnosis. We had no plan, except to keep the secret between the two of us.

Our emotional responses to this situation were different. When we looked into each other's eyes, I saw that Adam was panic-stricken by the confirmation of our suspicions. I didn't know what troubled him most; fatherhood or the fact that Big Daddy would make his rifle part of our immediate future. Either we would be standing with the preacher or Big Daddy would shoot him once the news came to light. My bet was on his getting shot.

I, on the other hand, had to conceal my joy. I was going to be a mother. We had conceived in love. It would be loved and it would love me unconditionally. I was elated. Unlike my other foray into motherhood, I would be able to proudly display my maternal status. I would participate in all the normal celebratory things that accompanied the impending birth of a child. Finally, I would have my own family unit. I was ready for that happy chapter in my life to begin.

TWENTY-THREE

Sunday Dinner

Another month passed and still no resolution existed for us. Consequently, my clothes got smaller, my appetite got larger and Big Mama's suspicious looks lingered longer. Time for stalling was up. We were forced to break our news to my family. We decided Sunday dinner would be the safest place for the exchange of this kind of information. I hoped the residual effect of Sunday preaching and the presence of the Holy Spirit lingered long enough for us to tell our truth without anyone getting hurt.

To say we were uneasy about this announcement was an understatement. I had traveled down the unexpected discovery road before, but from an entirely different direction. My first voyage to motherhood started from a place of predatory dominance. In contrast, our journey started from a place of purity and love. We promised each other that our love would last forever. Our commitment was about to be tested. We stood there, hand in hand, and let go of our secret.

We surveyed faces for immediate reactions. I was scared the woods in the back of the house would gain more fertilizer. I quickly formulated an action plan, based on necessity. In the past, I experienced the evil eye from Big Mama for something I considered minor. I braced myself for the verbal tongue-lashing that was primed and ready to spew like lava in our direction. Simultaneously, I stood ready to fling myself between Big Daddy and the pathway to the gun case in the event there was a need for Adam to run to the car. What we got was stone cold silence after the gasp that immediately followed our announcement. I looked at the floor in shame after I observed the pain that filled their eyes. All the lies and deceit that I visited upon my family found their way to the surface. My taste buds revolted when I remembered each unsavory syllable that passed from my throat to my grandparents' ears.

I could not have hurt my grandparents more if I ran over them with a car, backed up, and ran over them again. At least the trauma I caused would have been more visible than the internal rupturing of their hearts. They had done all they could to keep me safe and helped me regain my normal life. The sadness in their eyes expressed a level of disappointment I was not prepared for. Tears welled up in Big Daddy's eyes. He quietly detracted from the conversation and made his way outside to the porch swing.

Big Mama was the remaining risk factor. I was unsure of what to expect from her. She remained quiet for a long time before she asked, "What are y'all planning to do about this situation?"

Adam and I looked at each other as if the question was unreasonable. I realized we hadn't talked about what we were going to do. We shrugged our shoulders in unison, signifying to her that we were clueless, inexperienced children.

"Well, you'd better come up with something soon. Whether you are ready or not, that baby will make its appearance. It doesn't look like to me either one of you counted this cost when you started playing grown-up games with your bodies. How could y'all have been so irresponsible with your future?"

Big Mama paused for our response. Neither of us uttered a word. I prayed she was finished, but she wasn't. She reloaded her thoughts and started in on us again. She looked directly at Adam and asked, "Do you have a job?"

"No", was his answer.

Big Mama threw up her hands in exasperation and said, "Babies having babies. You don't have jobs or even a high school education. How do you plan to take care of an innocent child? You can't even take care of yourselves. Do you even know what it takes to be parents and raise a child?"

Big Mama looked directly at me and said, "Where are you gonna live? It certainly won't be here. That's not what grown people do. If you are grown enough to make a baby, then you should be grown enough to be out on your own."

I couldn't believe what I heard. I knew she didn't just say I couldn't live there anymore. We both were shocked into reality by those words. This was my home. I was gonna need help with my baby. The only babies I had ever taken care of were my dolls. They often ended up half-naked with arms and legs missing. That was not a good sign.

We stood there in silence until Big Mama spoke again. "Adam, I think it's time for you to leave. I can't guarantee your safety if my husband comes back inside this house."

We decided it would be best if we exited through the back door and walked around the house to Adam's car. The circuitous route kept ample distance between the two males. I kept a watchful eye on the porch swing where Big Daddy pondered in silence. How ironic that we took part of the same path that just months earlier I nervously watched Adam take with Big Daddy before he was granted the right to date me. Thankfully, my guest departed without incident.

On my way back to the house, I had to pass by Big Daddy as he sat quietly on the swing smoking his pipe. Our eyes locked for a brief second. I was overwhelmed with shame. I had to look away. I remembered when we sat on that swing shortly after my mother went to jail. He told me to move forward from my past situation and fill my head with knowledge instead of nonsense. Now my stomach was full of life, his heart was full of sadness and our home full of confusion. I was willing to bet he second-guessed his decision not to shoot Adam the day his car pulled up in our driveway.

TWENTY-FOUR

Acceptance

What a difference a day made. One day I was the apple of their eye, the next day I felt like the rotten apple. I was the same person they hugged yesterday; today I was untouchable. Each time we were all in the same room, conversations and looks were short and evasive. Our quiet dinners were dominated by the sounds of silverware clanging against glass plates and ice shaken around in glasses. But how had I expected them to act? Their reaction was typical for the enormous new wrinkle in their plans for me.

Our home life had been turned upside down since our pregnancy announcement. Big Mama eventually started our reconciliation process. She was concerned about my emotional state. After I assured her I was fine, I listened intently as she expressed how they felt. I learned during that conversation that fear, not rejection, fueled their actions. My fragile emotional and biological state was their biggest concern. I understood. I had not stopped long enough to consider anyone but myself. Neither of us was able to hold back the tears. My tears were of relief; hers were of concern for my future. After the initial shock and disappointment moved further into the past, it was clear that her love never wavered.

"I'm sorry Big Mama" was enough to put us back on track, but it was not that easy with Big Daddy. He continued to exercise the silence campaign. I wondered if things would ever be the same between us. Big Mama advised me to give him some time. I took her advice. I had other things on my mind. I was happy about where my life was heading. I had the love of my life and he was going to give me a family again. The love in my heart and the evidence in my body supported my position. But when I considered the disruption I caused in so many lives, my happiness bordered on being disrespectful.

Despite differing opinions about my maternal status, acceptance had to be the common denominator. There were too many decisions to be made and no room for unnecessary distractions. We didn't need futility as an ally at this juncture. With so many smiles to look forward to, I had to convince the prospective father and my family to agree with my joy. Whether he stayed with me or not, I would have and keep this baby. That was the only option I would even entertain.

I couldn't say the same thing for Adam. I could see in his eyes that being a parent did not bring him the same joy it brought me. On more than one occasion, Adam said he was not ready to be a father and questioned how I let that happen. Those words stung and ruptured my sense of security. I fought the urge to remind him that he was as responsible for the pregnancy as I was, but decided to hold my tongue. Each time Adam lashed out at me, I remained silent.

I chalked it up to frustration. There was no time to play the blame game. We had more important things to discuss. I didn't want to put too much more pressure on his already cluttered mind. I just had to be patient. He'd come around; I just had to wait.

TWENTY-FIVE

Not Just Yet

N o doubt it had been a struggle to get Adam to see things my way, but we were about to hear the baby's heartbeat for the first time. When Big Mama asked about prenatal care, our response was as empty as our pockets. We hadn't thought that far past the positive test results. I was just happy that in the face of these unfamiliar circumstances, the expectant father was right there with me. I hoped that hearing evidence of the life we created would bring him the same joy it brought me. Then, he would not be able to deny that we were a family.

For a moment I believed I had traveled back in time to the day my mother learned of my pregnancy and I heard the rapid string of nos from a distant room at the clinic. But in this version, the sound of high-pitched screaming was added to the memory. It took a minute for me to realize that it was not a memory. The screams were coming from me. The last conscious thought I remembered were the words "I'm sorry" before my mind retreated from reality. I woke up later in hospital garments. After the parade of medical personnel subsided, I was overwhelmed by the storm of emotions brewing inside.

All I could do was hold on to Big Mama and pray she would fix this for me. I wanted my baby back. I pleaded with her to make them bring it to me. But that would be an impossible task; there was nothing left. The fetus was disposed of as biological waste before I could even wake up from the extraction procedure. I had to leave the facility with an empty womb and broken dreams. I still hadn't been granted the privilege of motherhood. What was wrong with me that I couldn't do something as simple as having a baby? Two men plus two pregnancies equaled zero babies. My maternal math equation had been brutal.

I couldn't help but think I was punished for how I acted with my first child. I had not wanted it at all, and was glad when nature recaptured it. Its presence would have only perpetuated the pain its conception introduced. But I valued our love child from the beginning. I had so much stored up love waiting to be released. It had been beyond cruel for my baby to have been unceremoniously taken from me and thrown away with the trash. I wouldn't get to bury it or acknowledge it even existed past an arbitrary entry in some medical records. I should have been able to give it the same send -off and show of respect as the first child. If I thought it would help, I would have promised God anything to have not been punished in this manner. But destiny had applied its will and fate wouldn't alter my path no matter how much I begged. Big Mama rescued me from the madness of my gestational defeat and took me home.

Walking up those stairs no longer pregnant happened

under circumstances opposite from those I imagined. There was no crib to fill, no bottles to rinse and no smiles and coos to behold. I was alone in that room, in the bed where life had been conceived, feeling empty and numb. Big Mama could tell I was grieving and allowed me extra recovery latitude. I asked if Adam could spend time with me in my room. She consented. I quickly extended the invitation.

When Adam arrived, I was overjoyed. We could help each other maneuver through the healing process. I thought I had someone there who felt my pain and shared my grief as a parent. But something was off. His mood seemed less than warm throughout his visit. I wasn't prepared for the harshness he displayed. The sadness on my face was in direct opposition to the relief displayed on his. I realized that being faced with fatherhood hadn't been a positive experience for him. The possibility of being saddled with such huge responsibilities had changed him in ways I didn't fully understand. I longed for some genuine affection and understanding that he was unable to give. He was detaching from this relationship. I felt it. I knew I was losing him.

Forever and Ever

After the trauma of my loss, Big Mama allowed me to wallow in my sorrow and grief for about a week. She soon grew weary of my antics and told me I would just have to get over it. Her request seemed brash and heartless. Although it could have been categorized as cruel, it probably needed to be said. I had been shrouded in heaviness long enough. I wanted to get back into my normal routine. Going back to school would be the best medicine for me. But most of all I needed to see Adam. I knew I would be fine once we were together again. I was not prepared for the life lesson that awaited me in that hallway.

What I observed stopped me in my tracks. Seeing him posturing in the same manner as he previously did with me was an assault on my senses. Our eyes met, but instead of his coming over to greet me, he looked away. I knew he saw me, but appeared to want nothing to do with me. He walked in the opposite direction with one of my friends. I stood there in stunned silence. I didn't understand what just happened. He just loved me last week. We created and lost a child together. Sadly, that wasn't enough.

My immediate goal was to retreat to the nearest bathroom as quickly as possible. I wanted to avoid the embarrassment an emotional outburst would have caused. Once inside, I covered my mouth so the scream I wanted to expel remained trapped by my cupped hand. I sat down in one of the stalls with my mouth still covered and cried silent tears of love and loss. He promised me that our love would last forever. I believed him. I always thought forever was an infinite notion, but it ended one Friday between second and third period in a crowded, noisy hallway. I knew I wouldn't be able to face him again that day. I couldn't take any more rejection in Adam's version of forever. The dead flies description Big Daddy once spoke about, that characterized Adam's family's traits, were beginning to gather around his head.

I convinced the school nurse to call Big Mama because I was too heartsick to remain at school. Once again, I returned to the house of Big Mama emotionally battered, rejected and heartbroken. As always, she was there to provide the soft place to land without saying "I told you so" in voice or in her eyes. During the ride home, I recounted the reason for my distress. Big Mama listened quietly and allowed me to lay my head in her lap and cry as much as I needed. She just stroked my hair and hummed soothing melodies to replace the thoughts that roamed through my mind. Given the way I treated them, I knew I didn't deserve the level of compassion she conveyed. I gratefully accepted the gift and wondered what I would have done without her.

Once home, she ran a hot bath for me. We recreated a moment in time that I had forgotten how much I enjoyed. For a brief moment I felt like the innocent eight year old kid again. I enjoyed the time I spent with my grandmother as we washed away the awful events of that day. I thought the bath would work its magic and allow my mind and body to relax. It was impossible not to replay the morning's events. I convinced myself it was all a big misunderstanding. We just needed to reconnect. But somewhere deep inside I knew there was more trouble brewing than I wanted to acknowledge. I felt it when we last talked. His actions in the hallway confirmed those feelings. Even though our relationship was on life support, I believed a mouth to mouth and body to body transfusion would bring it back to life.

I was elated when Adam called. I thought it signaled his desire to patch up our differences. Initially, I did most of the talking. I tried desperately to keep the tone of the exchange as normal as possible. Eventually, the conversation took a detour from the happiness path I anticipated. The unwanted brush with fatherhood had been an eye-opener for him. He decided we needed to take a break. No matter how gently he put it, I didn't want to accept that he no longer wanted me.

The vision I had conjured up in my head about the longevity of our relationship crumbled before my eyes. Adam vowed to love me forever and I believed him. I gave him everything I had to offer. It was not enough. I was forced to watch those promises collapse on me like the debris from an imploding building. The difference between those blasts and my life was that the explosion was contained, and it remained within the bounds of the intended sector. The mental destruction I suffered went far beyond anything I could have imagined. It cancelled dreams, wounded hearts, eroded trust and rendered me as temporary as last week's headlines. My innocence died a long time ago, but Adam's betrayal assaulted my resurrected youth. I had lost more than he could begin to understand.

After that phone call, I curled up on my bed in the fetal position and cried. I was sick in my body and my soul. My body had not completely healed from the loss of my child before I had to deal with a broken heart. I ached at my core. After all the things I gave up for him, I became the momentary distraction Big Mama repeatedly warned me about. I had nothing new to offer after nature interrupted his fatherhood. We no longer had a bond. What remained between us was available to him from other willing sources. Adam took what I gave him, but he still left me behind.

Big Mama heard my muffled sounds of pain and quietly joined me on my bed. The look on my face told her that the conversation had not gone well. She remained quiet and allowed me to pour out my sorrow. She was not surprised by Adam's choice and couldn't mask her anger. She closed her eyes, shook her head from side to side and mumbled something under her breath. "Umph," was all I could decipher.

"Why don't I matter anymore? I was carrying his child. We were going to have a family. I always gave him what he wanted, so why doesn't he still love me?"

"I believe that was your problem. You gave away all your power to someone else until you had nothing left for yourself."

"I knew you wouldn't understand."

"I understand more than you think I do. I ain't been old my whole life. I understand having love from a man. How do you think your daddy and your aunts and uncles got here? I still enjoy a round every now and again, but you can't make it the entire basis of your existence."

Her comments surprised me. "Big Mama!" was all I could say.

She responded, "What? I'm still a woman and your grandfather is still a man, if you know what I mean." Her coy smile let me know she was not referring to Big Daddy's prowess in past tense.

She gently placed her hand into the center of my chest and said, "You must learn how to love the person in here, just as you are. You're not damaged, you're hurt and confused. Those things are not the same."

I looked down in shame. Big Mama placed her fingers underneath my chin and lifted my head. Looking straight into my eyes she said, "You must realize that your worth extends far beyond your own idea of who you think you are right now. Don't put too much weight on things that distance and time will render insignificant. You have the rest of your life to become who you were meant to be.'" Before she left the room, Big Mama said, "Get some sleep. Things always look better in the morning."

The conversation with Big Mama allowed me to release some of my anguish. Although she meant well, her advice wouldn't work for my situation. I knew what was best for me. Our love would prevail. Something as real as what we shared could not be reduced to nothing so quickly. I tried not to acknowledge the end of our union. I knew Adam loved me; he told me so many times. I wasn't going to fade away and become background noise. I was determined not to face the end of us. I was willing to offer him anything he wanted to stay with me. He had always been happy when our bodies connected. Because of that, I was sure he could be convinced to continue our relationship. If I could just talk to him again, everything would be fine.

I called Adam several times, but my calls went unanswered. When our paths crossed, he continued to divert his eyes. He found anything to command his attention except me. I was hurt by how easily Adam erased me from his list of priorities. As much as I tried to deny it, I was forced to accept the truth about our relationship. I had to face the inevitable. He had acted in a manner that was best for him. He made his choice and it was not me. I thought about how quickly three became two, then one. I was alone and lonely. There was no more us. I didn't know when I would be finished with that disappointment. I was not ready to let go yet. I was not ready to stop looking at the photos or considering myself Adam's girl. I could throw away the pictures and trinkets he had given me, but I was unable to shut off my heart.

Monday morning was coming and I didn't want to go back to that school. It was the last place on earth I wanted to be. Since truancy was not an option, I begged Big Mama to allow me to change schools. She refused. She told me that if I started running from the truth so early in my life, I would be running forever. I knew she was right, but I would have been fine with postponing the lesson.

More than anything in life, I was determined not to show on my face the level of hurt in my heart. I had to appear unfazed until I could regain my balance. I kept my head held high, my shoulders back and my focus on reaching my academic goals. I returned to the comfort associated with invisibility and watched as the old became the new. I allowed the cocoon that once sheltered my existence to enshroud me again. I roamed the halls in a zombie-like state, constantly stalked by memories that would not go away. They took every opportunity to disrupt any attempts I made to recover. I had to pretend the person I loved no longer existed, just as our baby no longer did. As before, Adam looked past me at some insignificant target in the crowded, noisy hallways. I wandered down those same hallways with empty arms, an empty womb and postponed dreams. Graduation couldn't come soon enough.

I hadn't been surprised in a long time, but a graduation card from my mother caught me off guard. I had not heard from her since she went to prison. I couldn't control the flood of emotions that seeped into my heart. I was still angry and hurt. Even while she was away in prison, she didn't want to see me. She obviously had nowhere to go, but that didn't matter. I still wasn't important enough to secure a small portion of her time. It seemed that when I needed her the most, she was never there. The card was as late as her attempts to reunite with me after she abandoned me at Big Mama's.

I looked at the handwriting on the card and remembered the note she left on the kitchen table. A chill ran through my body. I was suddenly transported back to the last day I saw my mother and the events that occurred after the discovery of my stolen innocence. I had irrationally accepted some blame for our separation. I believed that had it not been for my naiveté, we would have never been torn apart.

Big Mama had helped ease my guilt with her wisdom and I eventually accepted no blame for someone else's actions.

Over the years, attempts to keep the memories of my mother alive were spearheaded by Big Mama, but I refused to think about my mother past those random comments. I had buried most of my affection for her under layers of distrust and what I deemed as rejection from her. The card was undoubtedly a way to ease her guilty conscious and provide an avenue back into my life. The more I thought about the timing of the card, the deeper I fell into the chasm of anger from the past. For my own good, I decided not to borrow any more troubles. I had enough on my plate already. My focus had to be on my future, not my past.

TWENTY-SEVEN

Moving Forward

Iigh school was finally over and I was ready to explore the world that existed beyond the county boundary lines. Despite my failures in some aspects of my life, I heeded Big Daddy's advice and kept good grades. As a result, I garnered scholarships to several universities. I selected the one that took me the furthest away from my current home. My sanity demanded I remove myself from my valley of defeat and seek higher ground that would facilitate a new start. I needed to go someplace where no one knew me, had never heard of my current home and wouldn't know anything about my history. Completely starting over was what I needed most. I needed to leave the past as far behind as humanly possible. The less I saw reminders of what could have been, the quicker I would find myself again.

When I announced my college of choice, Big Mama couldn't conceal the sadness and concern that filled her eyes. She knew how badly I had been hurt and couldn't help but ask if my decision to go so far away from home was based on Adam and not entirely on the curriculum. I wouldn't admit it, but it was mostly my attempt to get over him. I felt there was nothing to tie me to that town. I was eager to see it grow smaller and less significant as I watched it change dimensions in the rear view mirror.

The morning of my departure finally came. I arose early to make final preparations. I hoped my grandparents knew I wasn't turning away from them, just the things that would keep me walking in place. I was scared, but would never confess my anxiety. I knew I needed a change. They had done all they could and had raised me as well as anyone could expect. It was time for me to stop pretending to be an adult and start my voyage into self-reliance.

As much as I didn't want to admit it, I was really going to miss the place I once referred to as my country home. I sat on the porch swing and reflected on those happier times that made me smile. Big Daddy came out on the porch, sat down beside me and began to smoke his pipe. Without saying a word, he made his famous smoke rings. I instinctively tried to capture them in my hands. I was unsuccessful. He chuckled at the futility of my quest and blew another elusive ring. When the pipe had no more smoke to give, he put his arms around me and hugged me tight. I didn't want him to let go. We shared a beautiful silence that spoke volumes into my soul. I knew his love for me was still there.

Right before I left, Big Mama gave me some unexpected gifts. I smiled when she placed the locket she referred to as a family heirloom around my neck. She impressed upon me the value of the necklace and the sacrifice of my ancestors who provided such a token to be passed down through my family. She then gave me a bank statement and a check book. I was blown away by the balance and immediately asked, "Where is the armored car that dropped all this money?"

"All that belongs to you. These are the benefits from your father. Your mother arranged for us to receive the funds on your behalf. We saved most of it for your college expenses."

I remembered one of the dreams of my parents; to save enough money to send me to college. Big Mama made sure she preserved that dream. I was both speechless and overwhelmed. She continued with her explanation. "Life is full of surprises. You never know from one day to the next what it will bring. Even when you think you know which way your life is moving, it changes. Things are not always as they seem. Just remember, life is not always an all or nothing situation. It's about balance. You must figure out what will be the equalizer for you."

Big Mama walked over and hugged me. When we let each other go she said, "We love you, but not as much as your mother does. Her love has no end. Someday I hope you find a way to forgive her. But that's a conversation for another time. Right now, there's a whole big world out there waiting for you. Now go and make all of us proud."

"Yes ma'am," was all I had left to say. I really was gonna miss my home and my family.

TWENTY-EIGHT

Searching

The college campus was its own micro city. The massive amounts of people were in constant motion like ants. It was the perfect place for me to hide from my old life. No one noticed me and I was content with my new surroundings. Having total freedom was something new and it took me a while to get use to the concept. Once I figured out that I was truly on my own, I became the typical sheltered college student who had been given their freedom. Academically, I flourished in my new environment, but socially, I was less successful. There were times when I looked over my shoulder and expected to see Big Mama following me from a distance. She was never there. I was in total control of when and what I did. That dynamic became a double edged sword. At times, I indulged in activities more frequently than a good reputation could absorb.

It was hard to understand the motives of my heart. Right when I thought I was marching to the beat of the right drummer, the music changed. I was left stranded and forced to figure out what happened to the familiar sound. I still heard music, but I no longer knew how to dance. My rhythm was gone. Because of that, I spent the bulk of my romantic encounters searching for what I experienced with Adam. I tried to find him or parts of him in every new physical encounter. My chest cavity was missing its vital organ, but I searched for relief from an organ located below the waist. My heart searched constantly while my body paid the price. I devoted the majority of that time comparing everyone to him in search of happiness. Sometimes I closed my eyes and pretended Adam was with me. When the act was over and my eyes opened again, I was still unfulfilled. I often found myself in the company of someone I barely knew. None were permanent attachments. They poured through my life like a sieve. One substitute survived a weekend trip to my home town, but didn't last too much longer after that. My motives for the visit were completely selfish. I wanted to make Adam jealous by showing him I had moved on with someone else. It didn't work. I still was not over him.

In moments of honesty and truth, I knew what I was searching for and why. Adam still had my heart. I needed to get it back. When he left me behind, I felt the same range of emotions that festered in me after my mother left me behind, only deeper. My mother inherently loved me because I was her child. Adam chose to love me because of the person I was. It often amazed me that the hurt from so long ago lurked just below the surface, ready to pounce when the moment presented itself. When I was with Adam, that anger was held at bay because he filled that void in my life. After he left me, a gaping hole remained where my heart belonged. I didn't know if it would ever be filled.

Corrosive memories haunted me and convinced me I

still wasn't good enough to be loved. Maybe if I still had one of them, Adam or the baby, I could have moved on. I would have been content with the part of him that existed in our child. Anything would have been better than having no man in my bed and no child in the crib. I didn't believe I would ever feel whole again. Big Mama tried to show me the light, but I shielded my eyes from her truths. I was convinced I knew what was best for me and ignored everything she warned me about. When I finally woke up from my puppy love coma, I realized the mess I had made of my life. The second chance I had been granted to live without the violation fruit tethered to my body was squandered. I had been freed to move beyond those 143 days, but chose to build my own lust-filled trap and fell into it without an escape route.

During one of our Sunday night calls, I complemented Big Mama on the long, loving relationship she had with Big Daddy. I wondered aloud why I was never able to settle down and function in a long-term relationship. I didn't know how she would respond, but it didn't take long for me to find out.

"Maybe it's because you settled for the next warm body that would fill the space between your knees, without regard to the matters of the heart."

The brutality of her honesty left me speechless. My prolonged silence offered an opportunity for her to continue with her assessment without my response.

"Have you ever asked yourself why you are still so mad

at him?"

"I already know the answer to that question. I am angry because of what he did to me. He broke my heart and treated me like I never mattered."

"I know Adam hurt you deeply, but you have to forgive him."

"Forgive him? Not after all he put me through. No. Not gonna happen."

"Not now, but someday it will. If not, you will continue to carry that hurt around, allowing it to block the path for love to find you again. You have to figure out how to forgive someone who didn't think they did anything wrong. Somehow, you've got to love yourself more than you dislike him. Forgiving Adam is the first step you need to take."

Disgusted by Big Mama's comments and how close they actually were to the truth, I abruptly ended the conversation. She didn't understand the depths of my hurt or could she appreciate how hard I tried to regain my balance. Regrets ate away at my soul and rendered me virtually lifeless. I was afraid to let my heart feel very much of anything anymore, but unable to quell the desires of my body. She insinuated I didn't love myself. Maybe that nosey, opinionated old woman was right.

TWENTY-NINE

Closure

After the last conversation with Big Mama, I dreaded our next exchange. I didn't refuse any phone calls, but I didn't make many either. Maybe that was the source of the guilt I felt when Big Mama called about Big Daddy. If I wanted to say goodbye to him, there was not much time. His chronic illness had progressed over the last couple of years and I was sure he was ready for his rest. I believed I had made peace with his condition, but when I saw him lying there, it broke my heart. His eyes lit up with recognition when he saw me. Those same eyes had shown me forgiveness and love during my foolish phase. Both of our eyes filled with joyful tears as we embraced. I sat with him for many hours during his last days. More love than I could ever imagine passed between us during that visit. I was glad I was able to say goodbye.

Although our minds were prepared, the shock of his passing still took our breath away. I didn't believe I would encounter a finer man. He took on the task of not only being my grandfather, but also my advisor, my father and my protector. He was my example of what a real man should look like. I realized how fortunate I had been to have shared my life with such a wonderful man. I knew he had loved me from my beginning to his end.

The memorial ceremony was befitting for how he lived his life. I was humbled by the number of well-wishers that visited our home to support Big Mama. Considering the gravity of the occasion, she showed incredible strength and grace. She consoled others more than she accepted solace for herself. I was not surprised. That was who she was. She had been that same person for as long as I could remember. There was no way she could change.

Although our home was filled with dozens of people, I had a feeling someone was watching me. When I turned around, I saw Adam. It startled me. The possibility of this reunion was never considered. After he walked over to me, I slowly scanned his face. I took in every nuance of it and marveled at how much he hadn't changed. It had been years since we were that close. I still remembered his smell, the strength of his hands, the shape of his mouth, the brightness of that smile and the power behind those eyes. His eyes still sparkled. I looked into them briefly, then quickly looked away. I was afraid to look in his eyes for very long. Those eyes and that smile had mesmerized me and wooed me until I was pregnant, broken and confused.

Adam sensed my apprehension and started the conversation by giving his condolences. I said nothing. I settled my mind and eyes on anything other than his face. I couldn't allow myself to get caught up in nostalgic feelings that were going nowhere. He grabbed my hand and I quickly pulled it away. I couldn't believe he had the nerve to touch me again. I thought it was very presumptuous of him to invite himself into my personal space. When I wanted and needed his touch, he refused. He didn't deserve to touch me now. Adam acknowledged my rejection of his actions. He raised his hands in the air, as if he was under arrest. Not wanting to cause a scene in Big Mama's house, we went outside. We began to walk, as we once did, around the yard. Those walks had been our bonding moments and the route we took was natural for us. A bit of nostalgia tried desperately to nudge its way into my mind. I rebuked those thoughts and kept myself closed off to any pleasantries of the past. For my own protection, I crossed my arms behind my back and clenched my fists as we walked. I didn't want any part of me to inadvertently connect with him. We stopped under a shade tree and Adam began the conversation again.

"How's college?"

"Good."

"You look good."

"I know."

We both laughed and relaxed a bit. After the laughter subsided, there was silence. Adam became fidgety as he struggled to find his words.

"Is there something in particular you want to say to me? If not, I need to get back inside with my grandmother."

He cleared his throat and finally said, "I'm sorry for how I treated you. You deserved better". He looked at me. I remained silent.

Adam put his hands in his pockets and looked down at the ground before he continued. "I was scared. I wasn't sure I could have been the father and the man our situation required. I turned my back on you and ran away when you needed me the most. I am so sorry. Can you ever forgive me?"

My mind stalled and my thoughts abandoned me. I forgot the words to the speech I had rehearsed. Before my mind could tell my mouth what to say, the word "yes" escaped from my lips. I was shocked when I heard it. I couldn't believe what I said. I looked around to see who had joined our conversation. It was still just the two of us. What had I just done? I always thought I wanted him to suffer, but I realized it was pointless. In order to keep him in bondage, I would have to remain there myself. I had been stuck there for too long. It was time to move forward.

"Thank you", were the next words I heard.

Adam moved closer and started to hug me. I was caught off guard. Fear caused me to stiffen up and maintain distance between our bodies. But I had to know if I still needed him; if I was able to let him go. In an attempt to get closure, I embraced him. When our bodies met, I felt something, but it was not love and longing. I felt my heart coming back to me. I pressed harder into him to ensure the transference was complete. Then I physically and mentally let go of that part of my past. I had forgiven him and had taken back my life power. I gave it away just steps from where we stood. It was befitting it was reclaimed there. When we disengaged, I thanked him for giving me my heart back. I left him standing in the yard puzzled about what that meant. I realized how wise Big Mama's advice had been. I had been holding on to that hurt for far too long. That chapter was almost closed.

When it was time to go back to school, I was a ball of emotions. My mind couldn't help but go back to the time when my own mother suffered from grief after the loss of her spouse. She melted away inside until only her shell remained. I knew the depth of the love and commitment between my grandparents. Suffering such a loss had been tough for me, but it undoubtedly was much harder for Big Mama. I offered to sit out a semester or to change schools so I could be closer to home. She would hear nothing of the sort. She assured me she would be fine. My gift to her and to the memory of Big Daddy would be to complete my education. The world was waiting on my gifts.

Things changed for me once I got back to school. I realized I had been living a marginal life bogged down with useless baggage and rubbish. I kept a cigar box full of photos and trinkets given to me by Adam. I hung on to those items as a way to stay connected to the life that had left me behind. I knew it was time to permanently close that chapter by disposing of the remaining tokens of my past. With purpose and decision, I ripped the photos and love letters into pieces. In celebration of my freedom, I threw them up into the air and smiled as the pieces fell around me like confetti. I felt lighter once I finally dropped the two hundred pound weight of my past. It was time for me to move forward. It was time to become the woman I knew I was meant to be. The reckless, childish behavior I once exhibited ceased and I concentrated on my educational aspirations.

My graduation celebration was more of an emotional experience than I could have imagined. I toyed with the idea of not participating in the traditional ceremony. I considered the accomplishment of earning a college degree the most important thing. Big Mama quickly set me straight on that notion. She explained that the festivities were not just for me, but for the people who sacrificed and supported me throughout the process. There was no way I could not honor them with the confirmation gesture. I represented the first person in my family to receive a college degree. My only regret was that Big Daddy would not witness my success, but Big Mama symbolically made his presence possible. Before the ceremony, Big Mama gave me Big Daddy's pipe. I was overwhelmed by the joyful memories of his love that it brought me. I tucked the pipe in the waistband of my pants and allowed him to escort me across the stage to accept my degree. With my diploma in hand I whispered, "We did it Big Daddy, we did it."

THIRTY

On My Own

My academic accomplishments opened up many professional opportunities. I selected a position that brought me closer to home. With this new job I was finally able to be out on my own and truly self-sufficient. It was very liberating being an independent woman and I truly enjoyed my current life. There had been a time when I doubted that I would recover from my past, but I kept working toward restoration. Now, it was my time to spread my wings and find my own path to happiness.

Big Mama visited a couple of times and made it a habit to call me at least twice a month. During one particular phone call, Big Mama informed me that she finally moved out of the old house into something more manageable. I was sure her explanation was partly true, but I was just as sure that since Big Daddy passed, the house that had been their home together was no longer a place of joy for her. I would miss visiting her there, but I understood. Big Mama rambled on from topic to topic, never seeming to land on the true reason behind the call. When she felt it was safe, she broached the subject of my mother again. I had a feeling in my gut that I would not enjoy her topic of conversation.

My gut was right. It was not the first time she had advocated on my mother's behalf. Each time she did, I made it clear I had no desire to open myself up to be hurt by my mother. I closed the door on that situation years ago, but Big Mama kept opening it. She could be like a dog with a bone when she set her mind to something. Maybe she thought that if she continued to bring up the subject, I would eventually concede. She underestimated me. I inherited a stubborn streak from her.

From what I gathered, my mother resumed the relationship with Big Mama and expressed the desire to reconnect with me. I was always mentally exhausted by any conversations we had about my mother. Those exchanges unearthed thoughts and feelings I felt were better left buried. I knew she meant well, but thought she should leave well enough alone.

"Your mother wants to see you. I think it's time you did."

"Well, I don't."

"Don't you think your mother deserves the same kind of consideration that you gave that no-good boy that nearly wrecked your life? How hard do you think it was for your Big Daddy and me when you broke our hearts with all that lying and fornicating you were doing? But at the end of the day, the love prevailed and we forgave you. That's what matters most. If you ain't made any mistakes that you don't regret, keep living."

"Wow, I can't believe what I'm hearing right now. I can't believe you went there. That was a low blow."

'No, baby, that was the truth. There is no substitute for family. You should learn to forgive even when you don't fully understand why some decisions were made. You seem to forget that everything she did, right or wrong, she did for you. Now you have the nerve to act like she's never done anything for you. Shame on you for acting like you're too good for your own mother."

"The shame shouldn't be forced on me, it's hers. You seem to be overlooking the fact that she abandoned me with you. Why didn't she want me to be with her? I'll tell you why. It was so that she could be free to run the streets and start a life without me. She wasn't thinking about me. When is she going to pay for how she treated me? For what she let happen to me? She didn't have time for me then, so I don't have time for her now."

"How can you be so selfish and unforgiving toward someone who sacrificed her own life for you? She never asked for anything in return. Life is too precious for you to act like this toward your mother. You better wise up and stop taking her for granted. Life is not promised to us from one day to the next. You should know how quickly life can change right before your eyes. You already lost your daddy and Big Daddy. Don't make your mother dead while she's still living. Please baby, open your eyes before life backhands you with a reality that will leave you with a black eye and an even bitter heart."

In an attempt to hide my anger, I took a deep breath before I responded. "Big Mama, I am trying to remain calm and respectful, but you are making it hard for me. Why do you always try to shove that woman down my throat every time we talk? If she is what you want to talk about every time you call, I would prefer that you don't call me anymore."

"You don't mean that."

"Yes, I do. Maybe if you would stop trying to run my life and worry about your own, we would be able to have a normal conversation."

The sternness in her voice let me know she was not pleased with my response. Without a doubt, she was standing with her hands on her hips. "You think you have it all figured out, don't you? You have a college degree, but you still need a lesson on life. I hope you are able to pay the price for the cost of that education. Life can change as quickly as the direction of the wind. One day you might find yourself in the middle of a storm with no shelter in sight."

I remained silent and breathed my objection into the phone.

"Maybe when you stop fighting the truth, you will begin to understand what I'm trying to protect you from. The best lesson is a learned lesson. I just hope you are prepared for the homework you'll be left with."

More silence dominated my side of our conversation.

"I love you baby and I only want what's best for you."

"I know Big Mama", was all I could say.

After we said our goodbyes, I thought about what Big Mama said. I understood how right she had been about forgiving Adam and I knew she was probably right about reconciling with my mother. But I would decide when the time was right for me; not her. I wasn't ready to let go of my hurt and my anger yet.

THIRTY-ONE

Time's Up

M ore than the customary two week time span passed
without speaking to Big Mama. I was fine with the
lack of contact. There had been a couple of calls the week
after our less than cordial verbal exchange, but when I saw
the area code, I decided not to answer the phone. The last
conversation had ended poorly. I knew I said some things
I didn't mean and was wrong for not answering that call.
I was trying to help her understand that I was a capable
adult who could make decisions about my life without any
interference from her. I was content to wait another week or
so before I called her again. Maybe by that time she would
have abandoned her attempt at orchestrating a family reunion between my mother and me. The consequences she
would face for her continued interference had been made
clear by my avoidance campaign. I was determined to stand
my ground and teach her a lesson about boundaries. I was
acting out of anger and would apologize later. In the meantime, I needed my space.

It had been really busy at work and I welcomed the
freedom of the weekend. I needed time to decompress. The
stack of unopened mail and the neglected household chores
made my list of priorities. I cleaned the house, top to bot-

tom, but ran out of inspiration when it came to the mail. I sorted through the pile and determined which items could wait. I couldn't decide in which pile the last itemed belonged. It appeared someone had taken the time to personally address the letter. The script seemed vaguely familiar. I thought it odd that the letter had no sender listed. My sense of urgency regarding its content classified it as just another piece of junk mail. It remained in the growing unopened pile for several more days.

Finally, I got around to opening the last of the junk mail. The plain white envelope gave no indication of the darkness it would unleash. I looked quizzically at the paper, as if the words were written in some foreign language. It took a moment for me to realize what I was looking at. A translator whispered into my ear the name of the dearly departed. What I held in my hand was the pronouncement of the end of my Big Mama's life. I was stunned beyond belief by the news and struggled to continue to breathe. The news had been as unexpected and life-changing as the loss of my love child. I did not want to accept either truth, but denial would change nothing. I had no choice but to surrender to the fact that Big Mama was gone forever. Opening a package that contained Big Mama's obituary was the last thing I expected on such a routine, non-eventful day.

I held the end of life announcement close to my chest and allowed the news to rest in my soul. Every particle of my being rebuked the notion to acknowledge this loss, hoping that avoidance would change the outcome. My heart was in such distress. I wanted to stay in factual limbo so the guilt wouldn't have a place to nest. Tears ran rampant and amassed in the crevice of my neck. I felt helpless and hopeless. I was forced to comprehend the brevity of life.

Bitter was the taste of death's victory. It forced its portions upon me and like it or not, I had to swallow. Just like the liver dinners Big Mama made me eat because they were supposed to be good for me, I had no voice in this situation either. I had to wash the bitter taste down with tears and digest it in its entirety. Even though we all will have a seat at the table, we are never really prepared for the meal. Death's table is always set, waiting for the guest of honor to arrive, yet we often believe the party will never be at our house, until it is. What added to my indigestion was the guilt that came along with the meal. I had cut off communication with Big Mama and treated her like I didn't love her. I realized that even in her last days, she tried to prepare me for this juncture in life. Maybe she knew her end was near and wanted to ensure I found the path back to my mother. Had this been the life change she spoke about? I would never know for certain. Given the outcome, that logic prevailed. I wondered if she had been trying to prepare me for what I never acknowledged as a possibility...life without her being there. Instead of embracing her reconciliation aspirations for me, I rejected those motives and her with indifference. She represented the good I had a hard time believing existed in the world and I treated her as if she didn't matter. What did that say about me as a person? Who was this person that I had become? That person bore no resemblance to the child that had been taught decency and values by her parents and grandparents. It was disgraceful how I honored their sacrifice.

As I thought about what had led to these unexpected consequences, I regretted what my foolish antics caused me to forfeit. I didn't even get to say goodbye because my heart had been full of pride and arrogance. I had pawned our relationship for a sense of control and I would be unable to redeem the ticket. I had taken her presence for granted. I thought there would be time to mend the rift between us. The last conversation had been so bad. I lashed out at her for doing what she always did. She spoke the truth I didn't want to hear. In return, I chose to abandon the one person who had always been there for me through the most difficult times in my life. I essentially told her I didn't want to speak to her again. I got my wish. I would never be able to hear her voice or see her face again; the earth reclaimed its elements more than a week ago.

Even though I recognized the futility of my actions, I ran to the phone with the announcement in hand. Through blurred vision I managed to dial the familiar number that connected me to my family. The operator's declaration that the number was no longer in service abruptly shifted me back to reality. The weight of the phone suddenly multiplied and my fingers had to just let go. The phone landed on the kitchen floor. My body and the life tribute quickly followed. Only one of the three survived the descent unbroken. It wasn't my physical body that was broken, it was my heart. Hoping that somehow she could hear me, I repeatedly said the words "I'm sorry." I remained on the floor at the point of impact and begged Big Mama for her forgiveness.

Across the floor lay the obituary that chronicled Big Mama's life. It had not moved from the spot where it landed earlier. I wanted to show my anger toward that evil piece of paper. I knew that it wasn't the paper's fault. It would have been the scapegoat I wanted to punish. Inevitably, the more I considered my options, the more valuable that paper became. I needed to appreciate the end of life announcement for the link it provided to Big Mama. Without it, the last memories of Big Mama would have to be the unnecessarily cruel words I said to her and the phone calls from her that went unanswered.

Because I missed the ceremony, I was left to imagine all the wonderful things that would have been said about Big Mama's life and the beauty of her existence. My eyes studied all segments of the tribute. I tried to commit to memory all relevant facts as I read the story of her life. Although beautifully written, the decorated sheet of paper did not represent the fullness of her life. It was the exclamation point at the end of her life's journey. All it could do was hit on the orchestrated highlights others wanted to include as a way to pay homage to our loved one. It would become a token and final memory others would take with them as a comforting souvenir. I scanned the list of loved ones selfishly looking for my name. It wasn't there. How could that be? How could the authors of this tribute have failed to acknowledge me and the special relationship we shared? Grandmother may have been her title, but mother had been her role in my life. How had I been grouped into the generic category of "grandchildren and host of family and friends"? Had I been there with my family, things would have been written differently, but the point was, I was not there. I had been home, trying to punish her for speaking her mind. I had forfeited the right to object to any decisions others made.

I remained engrossed in the contents of the tribute. No word was trivialized. After I viewed the sum of her life's work as it was expressed through the written words of others, I felt I had been in the presence of my grandmother. I observed unseen family photos that included images of my father as a child and grainy photos of several branches of our family tree. Through those photos, I got a glimpse into portions of my history and snippets of the life she knew before time and circumstances intervened. I was surprised and overjoyed by the inclusion of my graduation photo in the tribute. Remembering the joy of that day brought some badly needed comfort.

When the last word was absorbed and each picture had been reviewed several times, sadness began to creep in again. I knew that getting to the end of the inside pages meant there would be nothing left to do but close up the memorialized evidence of Big Mama's life and prepare to stow it away with my other highly regarded items. When I folded the paper over, I noticed there were more aspects of the tribute on the back. Normally, the back of these documents were blank, except for the customary identity of the officiant. But to my surprise, there was a poem, centered under a picture of my grandparents. After I read it, I was sure it was a message from Big Mama to me.

Unspoken Words

When there are no more words,
Our love still speaks,
Ours souls are free,
Our troubles have ceased.

When there are no more words,
Our memories will stay,
In the hearts of our loved ones,
In the recounting of our days.

When there are no more words,
No matter what you go through,
Know that we've just gone ahead,
We'll be there to welcome you.

When there are no more words,
And we feel so far away,
Let our love comfort you,
Today, Tomorrow, Always.

Once again, the depth of her love humbled me. I keeled over into a heap of sorrow and cried rivers of tears that left puddles of release and regrets. The cold floor was unwelcoming, but I stretched out on it anyway as if it had arms to hold me. I tried to manufacture comfort from a non-feeling inanimate object. But none came. I began to metaphorically compare the floor with my relationship with Big Mama. Why is it that we never notice the floor as anything other than something to walk on? Closer observation proves it is much more than that. It is the foundation that gives you support no matter how often you walk all over it. Sometimes it creaks and makes noise when the load gets a bit too heavy. Once the pressure is released, it bounces back and offers support, time and time again. Sometimes the dirt that is brought in on the floor can't be seen until it piles up or is viewed at eye level. The messes made on it are not always easily cleaned up. In my time of distress, the kitchen floor became the repository for my anguish. I shared my sorrow and tears with it until sleep manifested an escape. So I lay there in the symbolic bosom of Big Mama until the morning light signaled that the worst day of my life was finally over.

THIRTY-TWO

The Journey Home

I was exhausted and groggy when my eyes opened the next day and my surroundings became recognizable. The outside world continued to change. My world stood still. I heard and despised the joyful voices of nature. I deemed it insulting that an inconsiderate bird sat on my windowsill and disturbed the silence with its incessant chirping. How I wished it would move on since there were no worms living that far above ground. Mentally, I wanted to throw the first thing I could find at that noisy intruder, but I lacked the physical energy to move beyond where I laid. I was forced to endure the bird's offering until it completed its morning opus and mercifully flew away.

The events of yesterday continued to torment me. Unaware of any concept of time, I remained prostrate in the middle of my floor, trapped in the sorrow of yesterday. I struggled to find my mental posture. I was so ashamed of myself. I allowed those feelings to pull me deeper into despair. How could I move forward with the guilt noose pulling on my neck? No matter which way I turned, it choked me and I gagged from the pressure. I didn't know when and where I would find peace again. I needed someone to hold me and tell me everything would get better soon. Usually that was Big Mama's role. I didn't know who would be there for me now. My mother had reached out to me several times after being released from prison, but I rejected her. I was still so angry. My conflicted mind caused there to be no one to help me through the grieving process. Others had started their mission to recovery. I was sure no one wanted to start over with the painful journey on my behalf. I was forced to travel that path alone.

The confines of my apartment were suffocating me. I needed some fresh air. I had been recycling the pain and misery of my discovery for days. I continued to allow each breath to infect me with regret. I began to think about the trips to Big Mama's house with my father and the freedom I experienced during those times. I habitually rolled down the window and stuck my arm out. I liked to feel the coolness of the wind fill up my hand. Its invisible presence always pushed my hand backward. I could never grasp a handful of air no matter how hard I tried. That exercise in futility served no practical purpose, but it allowed me to focus on something simple and pure for as long as I remained mesmerized by the momentary attempts of success. I desperately needed to connect with someone. Thoughts of the trips with my father were enough to move me from that apartment to the open road.

Without a conscious thought of direction, I started driving and ended up at the old country house. I sat in the car for a while and took in all the sights, sounds and connections that surrounded me at that most special place. Instinctively, I found my way back home. I returned to the place where I found myself and lost pieces of myself. Right then, I didn't know who I was anymore. I needed to feel grounded and attached to my roots; to feel close to Big Mama again. It was my last option for redemption.

Although it showed signs of age, the house stood proud and strong; just like the woman who had been its matriarch for as long as I could remember. As I walked up the steps and onto the porch landing, the sounds of the wooden boards seemed to welcome me. I paused and partook of one of my most favorite spots in the world. I couldn't ignore the urge to sit in the porch swing. That swing had been our special bonding place. Both laughter and sadness congregated there. I was amazed it was still there and was hesitant to lower my body onto it. The creaky sound it made greeted me as it had so many times before. Slowly I relaxed the full weight of my body onto my old friend and gently pushed backward. With the weight of all the guilt I carried, I expected the swing to revolt, but it didn't. It allowed me to experience its gifts of momentary freedom as I relaxed and remembered all the love that was shared while we sat on that swing.

The gentle wind blew and stirred up bygone memories from dark places in my mind that I buried a lifetime ago. I tried hard not to remember that day, but the parallels of this moment intermingled with those from my past. Reality became cloaked with retrospection. I reached to wipe the phantom blood from my scraped knee. I felt a scar instead. I felt the haunting sensation of Big Mama's touch. It was joined by the echoes of familiar humming sounds that seemed to source its strength from the breeze. I repositioned myself on the swing, closed my eyes and nestled into her arms.

My life had gone through many seasons since then, but suddenly I was thirteen again. I was a child victim of abuse and unfortunate circumstances. I was neither equipped nor prepared for such an adult situation. I didn't know the value of a life or how the cruel thoughts and words of a child could plague me as an adult. At times I felt I was being punished for not valuing my first child, by being unable to have another one. I remembered how I hated that unborn child. I often hoped it would die, and it did. What kind of person did that make me? I thought I would have been happy when it died, but I had been conflicted by the outcome. It was innocent and I had been selfish and afraid. I could have sat there for hours enjoying the love I felt embedded in the swing, but I thought my peace awaited me on the inside of the house.

I made my way to the front door as naturally as I had done for so many years. I stood at the front door for a moment with the door knob in my hand and my eyes closed. I didn't know if I would truly feel welcome in the place where I came to experience restoration. Just as that thought finished, I heard in my mind the familiar voice of Big Mama telling me to wipe my feet off before coming into the house. I smiled as somewhere in time I heard myself say "Yes, ma'am". I pushed open the weather beaten door that guarded the entrance to my safe haven. Memories flooded my mind like the waters of Katrina. I closed my eyes and allowed numbness to be replaced by genuine feeling. I recalled the sounds and voices of those who took me in and loved me thru some of the most difficult times in my life.

Although the place was completely empty, I beheld all

the things that made that house a home. I saw pictures of family, the table where we had Sunday dinner, the rocking chair where I use to cuddle with Big Mama, the sofa where I had my phone calls from my mother. I heard the shushing sound she made when I disturbed her while she watched her "stories", the chiming of the mantle clock and the crackling sound of the wood burning in the fireplace. My nose was treated to the smells of my grandfather's pipe, biscuits and molasses, beans and cornbread, fried chicken, bacon, cakes and pies and Folger's coffee. I made my way through all corners of the room, where real living actually occurred, to the staircase, avoiding furniture that blocked my path, as if it were still there. On my way up the stairs I envisioned the photos along the bannister wall. I allowed my fingers to rub the holes left behind from where our family history was displayed.

The upstairs unearthed its own treasure trove of memories. I couldn't help but smile as I stood in the hallway that had been my gateway to many informational reconnaissance missions. I couldn't imagine my punishment had I ever been captured while eavesdropping into grown folks' business. Waves of conflicting emotions surrounded me while I stood in the door to my old bedroom. I began to see myself in stages; the innocent child who spent many carefree summers in that room; the abandoned child that longed for her mother for far too many years, the broken woman/ child that had been an expectant mother without clearly understanding the ramifications of someone else's decisions, the teenager who had discovered the many layers of love, the awakening of bodily desires, the finite notion of forever, the joy and pain of love and the healing that comes with time and distance.

For a brief moment, another memory flashed through my mind. I remembered the screams, the fear, the finality and the relief of that night. I immediately shook my head from side to side in an effort to dismiss any thoughts of regret. I couldn't change the past, yet something in me still held the sadness from that night. I knew what I said then, but the person I was trying to become demanded more from me. Maybe someday I would fully embrace the life lessons I had been taught while I lived there.

THIRTY-THREE

Unearthed

I made my way down the back stairs to the kitchen where I observed visions of myself standing on my tiptoes trying to reach the stove. I smiled. I remembered how I had labored under the tutelage of Big Mama's watchful eyes. I worked diligently to imitate her culinary skills. I loved sharing those times with her and learned well from the master. I breathed in deeply, trying to capture the fragrant aromas that escaped from those seasoned pots and pans.

I continued moving across the kitchen to the back door. I was caught up in a moment when my hand rested on the door frame. That very door had witnessed Adam's sneaking into the home the night I chose to give myself to him. It had also been his avenue of safe passage after our pregnancy announcement. My life had shifted drastically between the opening and closing of that door over such a short interval of time. I wondered if I would have done things differently. Perhaps, but I could honestly say I would not have changed the joy and the sense of beauty and belonging I felt with Adam. My only regret was my not being mentally prepared for what came at the end of love.

I slowly opened the back door. The hinges loudly noted their displeasure from being disturbed. The open door brought much-needed freshness to the house. The reminders of my past found an escape route down the back stairs. They were committed to nudging me in the direction of yesterday. Looking out the back door brought back memories that were buried years ago. My mind seized at the moment my body was freed from the destruction caused by one inhumane action. The haunting visions and screams that couldn't be contained in the upper rooms invaded my mind. I covered my ears to insulate myself from the internal noise. It got louder. I wanted no part of those memories. I quickly exited the house to escape the reach of those skeletons.

I stood in the middle of the back yard and removed my hands from my ears. The voices from the past continued to stalk me from all directions. I heard my name whispered by the winds and trees, wondering if I was the same lost soul who once scrambled to exit the place of shadows and secrets. I was entranced as I headed across the yard in the direction of the place I vowed never to return. I felt powerless to reject the invitation when the past beckoned me to come closer. When my feet realized they were at the edge of the woods, they rebelled. The rest of my body agreed. The last time they came in contact with the dark, damp soil of my past, they were going in the opposite direction. In contrast, my mind and body agreed that running away was not what was best for me. I hoped the hidden place in the woods contained the salve that would heal some of my hidden wounds and ease part of the suffering I had endured for far too many years.

With all the courage I could muster, I boldly stepped through the tree-lined portal into my past. I retraced my steps to the place where I hoped my healing could begin. I didn't remember much about that entire episode, but I did recall the spot was marked by a tree with a cross carved on it. Recognition of the landmark took my breath away as I began to acknowledge what I had avoided out of survival. I had been wrong about the value of the life that peacefully rested there. It was time I accepted my child. It bore no shame, caused me no harm and was as much a victim as I was. The disdain I felt for my baby was a combination of misplaced aggression and fear. Back then, I didn't know if I could have loved it, given the nature of its origin. Standing there I admitted to myself that I loved it from its first fluttering movement. After going thru the disappointments of an unrealized bundle, I often wondered if I was being punished from not cherishing the child I didn't appreciate. All I could do was admit my mistakes, ask for forgiveness and finally put this matter to rest. The residual effect of that open wound had troubled my soul and fueled bad decisions in my life for far too long. Closure, was long overdue.

Kneeling at the spot where I predicted its grave to be, I surrendered my anger and my guilt to the heavens as my tears watered the earth. I never imagined the freedom I would feel by deciding to just let go. Pounds of dead weight vacated my being and space was made for something good.

With that being finished, I decided it was time to name my child. Below the cross I carved the name "Agape". If anyone happened to find our special place, they would know love was there.

I suddenly realized that had it not been for Big Mama, I never would have had an opportunity for freedom. I had wanted all traces of its life to be thrown away in those bed coverings. I silently thanked her for her wisdom. I sat quietly next to the tree and absorbed the beauty and peacefulness of the surroundings. Understanding it was my final visit, I placed one hand on my heart and one on the heart on the tree. Then, I said my final goodbye. My first child and I were both free from my misgivings and united by love.

When I finally exited the woods, I didn't run, I walked. The sorrow from that part of my past had finally been released. I had made peace with the child I was and the one that was lost. The rustling leaves of the trees and the high-pitched sonata of the cicadas serenaded me with admiration. I lingered in the back yard after exiting the woods. I tried to capture all that was available for me to store in my soul for future strength. I knew it was my last trip to what I once referred to as my summer home. There was nothing left for me there. I relished in the faint sounds of laughter and Big Mama's stern voice telling us to stop running through her clean sheets. I saw visions of me and my friends playing hide and go seek, walking on tin stilts, prematurely raiding the vegetable garden and helping white-haired dandelions find their place in the wind. All those things represented the joyous times of my youth and the good life I had spent there with my grandparents.

After making my way back around to the front of the house, half of me rejoiced, the other half remained unsettled. I felt released, but not forgiven. I hadn't emptied the buckets of confusion trapped in the wells of my mind. I questioned the divine purpose of my visit. I asked myself if I would have been able to move past the hidden sorrow without the intervention in the woods. My answer was no. I had unintentionally bumped into closure searching for forgiveness. Both were needed, but only one was fulfilled that day. The one thing I wanted most had not been accomplished. I still felt distant from Big Mama. I feared she didn't know how much I truly loved her and how sorry I was for the words I didn't get to share.

It had been good for me to feel the safety from being home, but I knew my time there had come to an end. On the way to my car, I grabbed more memories for safekeeping. I recalled the sights and sounds of the country and the faintest whistle of the trains destined to flatten our pennies. I smiled at our childish antics and tried to count how much money we had sent down the tracks.

Walking away was more difficult than I could have imagined. I understood the distance between this house and me would only grow greater. I balked at the concept of never returning, but I refused to depart with sadness. Love had lived there, I had been its beneficiary, and in the grand scheme of things, nothing but the love had ever really mattered. As I turned to say my final goodbye to my childhood home, my eyes couldn't help but find their way back to the porch swing. Even though there was no wind, the swing was slowly moving back and forth. I waved in its direction and said "I love you too Big Mama". I wanted to believe her presence had been closer than I realized.

THIRTY-FOUR

Evolution

It had been days since returning from the old house and I still could not shake the sadness that engulfed my spirit. While I had made peace with my first child, I still needed to be forgiven by Big Mama. I was unsure of how that could happen. No amount of standing over her grave or profuse praying would elevate this loss to a Lazarus situation.

My grief was funny and unpredictable. It didn't show on my face as the acid of loss ate away at my soul. It consumed me and dimmed my inner lightness in an effort to fuel its greedy existence. With each passing day, I fought hard to distance myself from it and return to what I considered normal. Most days I struggled to don a professional appearance after waking up with swollen eyes that were matted shut after a nocturnal emission of salty tears. My eyes were not black as Big Mama had predicted, they were red and my mind was filled with blues. Any progress in the direction of normalcy that occurred during the day was wiped away each time I returned home. Most thoughts and actions eventually returned to guilt and sadness. Eventually, work became no match for grief either. It gobbled up the fruits of that labor and spit out unemployment. It had me all to itself. Before long, grief gave birth to its love child, depression. That newborn had a voracious appetite that fueled its subtle replication process. It took over where grief left off and continued to stroke my tortured soul. My body and mind needed comfort and I succumbed to the first forces that could satisfy those requirements.

Depression made it easy for me. It allowed me to wallow in my sorrow while it continued to keep its presence inviting. It required nothing, expected nothing, offered nothing, and criticized nothing. It loved on me and encouraged me to stay with it a little longer. No one understood how I felt and depression told me it was OK to have it around. We cohabitated until I didn't recognize myself. I became content with going days on end with hair that resembled tumbleweeds and a bodily odor that I never knew was humanly possible to exude. I became a prisoner of my own mind, space and time. I didn't eat regularly, entertained irrational thoughts regarding the importance of my existence and cried. I allowed depression to stay with me and play with my thoughts as it matured inside me.

I recognized depression as the same beast that held my mother captive and allowed her to be lost in its arms. The same inability to function she exhibited after the loss of my father was lodging within me. I remembered clutching her as she lay in her bed weeping. I tried desperately to hold on to the pieces of her that I needed. I remembered the feeling of her latching onto me as if she feared I would go away too. I had been her lifeline and the reason she fought so hard to stay connected to something loving and familiar. For a while, I had been her rock on the shoreline of uncertainty. Eventually my anchor had not been enough to conquer the demons that infested her mind. She let me go to save me. Who could save me now? I had no one. I questioned if I deserved to be saved.

There was a constant tug of war going on inside my mind between truth and conjecture. Dark forces inside me fought for the empty space I carried around every day. Some days I was startled into reality after spending joyful time with Big Mama in my dreams. We were together at the old house. I was happy and content in her presence. I pleaded with her not to leave me each time she slowly faded away. When I was awake, our connection was lost. I often begged sleep to rescue me from the sadness of those days.

There were some nights when sleep eluded me and took away my opportunity to dream about happier times. Daybreak arrived and I laid there asking myself why I couldn't close my eyes. Why couldn't I get some relief from my own mind? Big Mama often said it was always darkest before the dawn, but for me, the darkness was unending. I experienced no light. When nature dictated all should be silent and peaceful while the refreshing process took place, the inner turmoil held me captive and churned uncontrollably. It wrestled with my peace and pierced my thoughts until the newness of another day broke free. My mind became layered in darkness before the light could shine through. I eventually expected nothing but the same each day and was unbothered when I was rewarded with those expectations.

Other days I spent countless hours just holding myself while I rocked forward and backward with no purpose. I stared into oblivion through vacant eyes and waited for comfort and clarity to come. Maybe they'd find me tomorrow, or the day after that, or maybe even the day after that. It really didn't matter when or if they chose to show up; my reality would remain the same. I would still be there alone. No one would even notice my absence from their lives.

In my younger days when life pressed up against me, I often sought comfort in the ample lap of Big Mama, where love engulfed me thru the smell of Ponds cold crème and songs from breaths that held the distant aroma of Folgers coffee. I never understood how much her unconditional love would become the foundation for a well of hope whose bucket and rope were never too empty or too short. How I longed for those carefree days and the unlimited amount of love that guided my life.

I needed inspiration to find myself again. I had a cohabitation agreement with depression and it would keep me wrapped in its expansive arms for as long as I stayed there. Contentment became my enemy. I was dissolving away like alka seltzer in a glass of water. I felt powerless to stop it. When the fizzing sound stopped, I feared it would be the end of my sanity.

THIRTY-FIVE

Intercession

I questioned my ability to move forward after I tried for weeks to get back to what I considered normal. I didn't see the point. The outward proof of my worth, my babies, Big Mama, even my mother, was all gone. I was without a lot of things. I lacked direction, love, ambition, pity, anger and anything that made me know I was still alive. I didn't care much about anything that tempted me to move beyond the confines of my bed. I often told myself to get out of bed, but never did. My reality wouldn't change if I sat on the couch in the lonely apartment instead of lying in the bed. I felt dead, but just hadn't been buried. I saw no reason to get up from my pillowtop grave. At least it wanted me. It was not bothered by my presence. Big Mama often talked about the restorative magic of nighttime and moments of clarity that followed after a good night's sleep. I had been sleeping for days but restoration still avoided me. Nothing was clear anymore.

My mind could control many things, but it could not control nature. No matter how I tried to avoid it, I had bodily functions that could not be denied. I couldn't remember the last time I consumed anything other than water. I needed to eat something. The groaning and gurgling sounds emanating from my stomach signaled agreement with that decision. Like it or not, the kitchen had to be my destination.

As I passed the bathroom, my eyes caught a glimpse of a lighted fragrance bulb blinking near the vanity. I was certain the bulb had burned out already and the fragrance evaporated from it long ago. Once I entered the room, the aroma was not the smell of jasmine or lavender, but of coffee. I thought about how strange it was to buy a room refresher that smelled like that. Surely the smell was the result of a burning refill that needed to be replaced. To the touch, the unit was cold. It would have been impossible to cause fragrance to be cast across any space. I was puzzled. I was certain the light had flickered on and off.

When I changed my focus from my momentary investigation of the great fragrance caper, I caught a reflection in the mirror that was not of me. I had not recently worn braids or glasses, my face was not that square and my nose was not that size. I flinched in recognition of the image staring back at me as my senses were being bathed in the overwhelming smell of coffee. I slowly reached forward to touch the distorted reflection of what I logically knew should have been myself, but appeared to be Big Mama. I clearly understood the impossibility, but still hoped to feel the warmth of the touch from gentle fingers I remembered from long ago. In my search for reconciliation, my fingers abruptly felt the rigidity of the cold surface that kept me away from the one thing I needed most. I longed for the connection from someone who loved me and knew how to comfort me until my pain, anguish and fear moved on to their next victim.

To my amazement, the vision moved. A hand reached

out to meet mine. A loving smile and words from familiar lips said, "I love you baby. I know you didn't mean any of those things you said. You were still hurting. I already forgave you. Everything is going to be alright. Your babies are here with me. I'll take care of them until you get here. But right now, you've got to start living again. You deserve some happiness."

The image of Big Mama slowly faded and the reflection transformed into my own likeness. My fingers remained pressed against the glass until I couldn't physically hold them there any longer. Like raindrops making their way down a window, my fingers found their way to the end of the mirror, past the faucet and eventually found their resting place near my heart. I stood there in total disbelief. I didn't know whether it was fact or fiction; if it was a dream or reality. I didn't know whether I should laugh or cry; whether I should embrace the moment or discount it as an inappropriate gift from my grief. I gladly accepted the gift. I had been forgiven. Big Mama told me herself. I wrapped my arms around myself and rocked from side to side with gentleness and love the way Big Mama use to do. I cried for the joy that quickly surrounded my being. Relief came in knowing that the babies I grieved were fine. Big Mama had experienced the same type of loss and understood the need to ease my mind.

The tears fell harder and faster as I cried from the depths of my soul. They changed from constricting to cleansing. I was finally able to release my anguish back into the universe. I couldn't carry it any longer. It had gotten too heavy. In the distance, I heard the clock chime six times. It was morning, and yes, my cleansing had begun. The solace of the morning and the intervention from Big Mama had given notice to squatters in my spirit that check out time had passed for anything that sought to hold me down. The grief hotel was permanently closed.

Old Wounds

After all the heaviness of Big Mama's passing, the trip to my summer home, and the haunting vision of Big Mama, I was ready for some lightness. Everything about my current surroundings constantly reminded me of loss and fought against my recovery efforts. A layer of sadness covered everything around me. It felt like I was living in a tomb. Out of necessity, I knew I had to move in order to move on. Once I became committed to the process, it didn't take long for my plan to come to fruition. I was excited for the opportunity to start over in new surroundings with a refreshed outlook on life.

In the midst of my recent loss and my desire to move my life forward, I came to the realization that it was time to reconcile the relationship with my mother. I always thought she owed me an apology, but in reality, I needed to forgive her, with or without it. I had learned from experience that the forgiveness was not for her, it was for me. I had to forgive her for everything, real or contrived, before I could finally let go of the difficult parts of our past.

While she was locked up for all those years, she forbade Big Mama from bringing me for a visit. She did not want to be viewed by her daughter as if she were some inhuman subculture of nature that was no more important than an animal at the zoo. She didn't ever want prison life to appear normal. In my mind, those instructions represented another form of rejection from her. I considered it equal to what I felt when she abandoned me at Big Mama's house. I hadn't felt like a priority in her life after my father died. I carried that insecurity into every relationship I tried to form. I didn't know who would want to be with a person whose own mother didn't even want to be around; whose own mother didn't feel was a valued treasure. Those shackles had weighed me down for far too long. I believed she had the only key that would free me from myself. I needed her help to heal the broken child inside. But if we never communicated our true feelings, hurts, questions, and fears, healing could never begin. Too many unspoken words between us required a meeting with our vocal chords.

It had been a long time since I had been face to face with my mother. I often feared I would be unable to recognize her if I passed her on the street. That fear quickly subsided when I saw her walk thru the café door. She looked the same, but different. Before our eyes could meet, my eyes were immediately drawn to her hands. Somehow, I expected them to still be stained with the red tint of blood as they were the last time I saw them. So much had changed about her physically from the woman who brought retribution to my abuser and defended my honor to the utmost. Her face showed a more seasoned version of the person I remembered. Looking into her eyes, I saw fragments of the same troubled eyes that had locked onto mine as the police car moved beyond my sight. However, beyond the sadness, I saw the fullness of the love I remembered from our early years. It made my heart smile. Her love for me was still evident.

Although I had every intention of being guarded during our first encounter, parts of me softened as I genuinely realized I truly missed my mother. I was so happy to be with her again. No matter how many times I had told myself I could make it without her, I still loved and needed my mother more than I had been willing to admit. In order to get the most out of the reunion, I had to lean into the moment and accept the universe's offering without fear of relational remission. I was ready for my soul to have peace.

Our conversation had instances of silence as we struggled to find a common core of topics. We initially avoided any words of substance and chatted about generic subject matter. My mother's comment about my picking up Big Mama's coffee-drinking habit made us both smile. It served as the bridge to the discussion of her passing. My emotions were still raw and I wasn't sure how long I could keep my composure while discussing such a sensitive topic. It was apparent from both of our reactions that the loss of such a vital piece of our family would not easily be overcome. My mother revealed she had sent Big Mama's end of life announcement to me. She expressed her bewilderment over why I hadn't attended her funeral. Those words felt like a kick to my gut. The high horse I rode in on had been reduced to an ass when the irony of this revelation became apparent. I had been angry at my mother for years for not being there for me. She had witnessed first-hand how I failed to be there for Big Mama. It would be hard to determine whose immoralities were greater. My level of intolerance diminished as we got deeper into our reunion. We were standing on level ground and our conversation could be one of commonalities, not superiorities.

For the longest time I blamed my mother for so much that had gone wrong in my life; some legitimate, some not. I wanted so much for her to want me in her life that I tried to protect her feelings regarding her boyfriend. In doing so, I exposed myself to a dangerous liaison that culminated in my life being changed forever. I had been forced to carry around rancid secrets that constantly interjected themselves into my quest for rebirth. For years I had wondered about my mother's swift action against my attacker. I hoped to finally get answers. No doubt he deserved every ounce of pain and anguish he experienced; I wondered why the punishment had been so harsh and so quick. Within three hours of my confession, his sentence had been executed. The separation of his manhood from his body had been the business she attended to after dropping me off at school. So much about what transpired that day existed beyond the scope of my knowledge. My questions regarding that episode should not have been unreasonable or unexpected. Pain cascaded down her face. Her body language spoke in code to her senses. It caused her to shift nervously in her chair while more truth was unearthed. I expected a detailed version of her rationale. Instead, I discovered we shared a deeper connection.

THIRTY-SEVEN

Counterparts

M y mother had a story of her own to tell regarding the explosion of rage that poured from her as she executed the sentence of my abuser. Her story was similar to my own in many aspects, except for its outcome. The anger that festered inside her for decades found its way to validation. After being disappointed that she was not believed, she ached from feeling ostracized by her own family. Neither she nor the violator ever received the justices' each deserved. He was allowed to continue to sow his seeds of destruction and she remained stuck in an infinite loop of disbelief and pain. Conversely, my mother never once questioned my truthfulness and exacted the punishment she viewed would have been appropriate for anyone who willingly hurt a child in that manner. She had not been certain if I had been his first, but she made sure I was his last.

The burden and shame she had carried around from her youth was lifted by her act of retribution. Her actions somehow healed the wounds of the child who had been forced to choke down her truth in shame. My mother had been adamant that I lived with Big Mama and not her family. I understood why. I would not have received the love and compassion needed to survive my ordeal with some modicum of normalcy. She had first-hand knowledge of the tenderness my grandparents would have shown. She had felt so alone during her ordeal and was thankful for the true love of the kind man she found in my father. He had softened her heart and helped heal parts of her brokenness with more love and patience than she felt she deserved. That depth of caring could only have come as a result of nurturing from a woman who had invested her own core values in her children. I could not have survived had it not been for the choices my mother had made on my behalf. For that I owed her my love and respect.

After hearing her story, my mind reflected back to that horrible time years ago. The pain associated with that time found its way to the surface. The molestation stones had dropped into the water of our existence and caused a ripple effect that overshadowed portions of our lives. Concentric circles were formed when our history of abuse was exposed. We had lived parallel lives during parts of our childhood. I didn't know if I could have been as strong as she had been forced to be. She had to constantly see the person who shattered the joy and freedom of the years that each child deserved. I will be forever grateful for the unselfishness of her sacrifice. Big Mama had known both sides of her story and that wisdom had directed her to encourage our reunion. She knew our developmental years had many things in common and we needed each other to survive the next phases of our lives.

I understood how history changed people and personal

choices determine if it will be for better or for worse. In my case, I chose to allow history to make me better. I had spent too much time objecting to my history without realizing that it was just that, history, and its rightful place was in the past. It had been bad then, so why would I continue to give it a second chance to wreak havoc on our lives. My version of the truth and my notions of disrespect had not been based in fact. They had been mostly caused by the end of understanding being manifested in a lonely, confused child. Now, I had to be the person I thought my mother should have been, but my life couldn't be directed by her life. I was forced to downplay her blame and stand in my own truth. I had to finally acknowledge the unmerciful influence she had on my life, even in her absence, but own my actions and my mistakes. We both shared the same fears, and in some ways, walked the same dark path. We were led by open wounds that never healed and resulted in our acting outside of our values, in search of relief. It became increasingly apparent that we still needed each other.

It seemed that we talked for hours and both of us enjoyed the progress we made. Neither had known what to expect, but agreed it would not be our last meeting. We had started a new chapter in our lives. We accepted the failures and revelations that held us back and propelled us forward. There would be no happily ever after unless we were both willing to put in the work and allow our hearts to heal naturally. Our mother/daughter relationship had been aborted decades earlier and we had to play catch up. The length of the disjointed path we were required to travel appeared daunting. We committed to take one step and one meeting at a time toward bridging the gap between us. This time when we embraced to say goodbye, time and distance were not waiting to separate us.

THIRTY-EIGHT

Look Up

My alliance with self-pity gradually ended. Because of my neglect, it moved on to another victim. I wouldn't miss it. I felt myself peeling away the layers of defeat and watched it fall away like the withered leaves from a maturing bouquet of flowers. The hollowness from losing Big Mama was replaced with courage. I began to see beyond what was and what never would be again. I turned my attention to what was to come. I had to find my own way and to find my light again. I was content to patiently exist until the unfamiliar became familiar and I regained my balance. After I became centered, the direction I chose to take led me to a new place and a new beginning.

Getting acclimated to new surroundings was challenging, but necessary in order to start over. A fresh start in a new city was what I needed. Big Mama had given me permission to move forward and that was what I needed. One thing that I had inherited from my Big Mama was a love for good coffee. Remembering the days of old and the first time I tasted that caffeinated wonder of nature, made me smile. There had been many cups between the small saucers that were filled with a concoction that was more milk than coffee to my current morning ritual of a strong cup to start my day.

Big Mama once told me that love comes best when people take time to get to know each other beyond the physical attraction. She always encouraged me to get to know and love myself before I tried to bring someone else into my life. She should know. She had been by my side through the revolving door of companions I discussed with her during my wayward college years. She understood the reasons behind my actions and was there for me, offering love, patience and words of wisdom. She knew I had been broken in so many places and required time to heal. After I reclaimed my heart from Adam, I vowed to take it slow in the relationship category. Those were my intentions. I just wasn't counting on that wonderful specimen of a man I encountered that day.

I had frequented this coffee haven many times, but that visit would be one I would not easily forget. Standing behind a well-dressed, well-groomed, good-smelling man unexpectedly stirred something in me, even though I could only see the back of him. Thank God for small favors because if his face was anything like his body, I was in real trouble. I caught a glimpse of his profile and my body's reaction was justified after I partook of only a small portion of him. The clerk loudly cleared her throat in an effort to refocus my attention from the man to the coffee. Feeling slightly embarrassed for consuming the eye candy, I began to fumble through my purse for money to pay for my drink. The clerk informed me that the gentleman in front of me had already paid for my purchase. I stopped grinning long enough to thank the clerk for the coffee and quickly tried to catch another glimpse of my benefactor. To my disappointment, he would have to remain a mystery for a while longer.

For more than one reason, the coffee shop became my favorite decompression chamber. From my favorite table I could relax, people watch and take in the vibe of the surroundings. Several weeks passed and I still thought of my brief encounter with the mystery man. I fantasized about what it would be like to see his entire face, hear his voice and feel his touch. I was sure any type of physical connection would be electric. The fleeting glimpse of his profile had only whetted my appetite. I was ready to feast on the entire meal. The universe must have been reading my mind because the mystery was solved right in front of me.

When I realized he was the one I had been fantasizing about, I was at a loss for words. My eyes methodically surveyed the entire landscape of his body and finally settled on his face. His baritone voice and the smell of his cologne temporarily put me in a trance that would have rivaled any hypnotist. I didn't even remember his asking or my accepting his invitation to join me. I couldn't take my eyes off him and nearly burned my tongue on the hot coffee. The dialogue going on in my head kept urging me to remain calm and not act as if he were the only cup of water at the first rest stop on the other side of the desert. The ocular meal was not one-sided; his attention was not totally centered on my face. Since I understood fleshly fascination, I suppressed the urge to inform him that my breasts didn't have eyes. They had come a long way from my youth. I smiled as the memory of my first bra hanging on the line with Big Mama's flashed thru my mind. Eventually, I learned that his

167

name was Ben. Between pleasant conversation and genuine explosions of laughter, we enjoyed each other's company and made plans for a formal date. It took about a week for our magic carpet ride to begin.

Getting to know Ben had been amazing. He appeared to be the perfect guy for me. He was a salesman who traveled extensively for work, but said he always wanted a family and a stable relationship. He was still searching for something he had not been able to find yet with the women he had dated. He was looking for someone special to give him a reason to take a desk job. Ben was well-spoken, charming, generous and respectful. Everything we did was vertical and filled with a mixture of meaningful discussions about current affairs and playful banter about our favorite childhood obsessions. No topic was off limit, felt awkward or had gone unanswered. I learned that he valued family above all because he too had lost one parent and had been estranged from the other for quite some time. He confided in me how he had dealt with his own grief and longings. I was honored that he trusted me enough to open up about such intimate details of his life. He trusted me with his emotions and that was a major component of building any successful relationship.

The more time we spent together, the more determined, I was not to let that prize catch off the hook. Between the flowers being sent to the office, the candlelight dinners, the extended phone calls, and random gifts "just because", he was winning my heart. I was getting close to taking a giant step toward committing both my mind and my body to this man. Being in his presence was intoxicating and I looked forward to each refill. Somewhere inside my head I heard the voice of Big Mama. Her words were repeated like a broken record each time I excitedly told her about new gentleman callers. "Take your time, baby. That ain't the last man God created. If that one moves on without you, trust me, there'll be another. Don't be in such a rush to open up your pocketbook and pass out your change. That is not the place of love; you have to look above the waist for that. Once you find it, everything below the waist takes on a different meaning. One day you are gonna realize you are worth more than the space between your knees."

THIRTY-NINE

What's Been Cooking?

The relationship with my mother gradually became a source of strength for me. We talked once or twice a week and used that time to speak openly and honestly about our past. I told her about Adam; how deeply I fell for him, the child we lost and the difficulty I faced with letting him go. My level of comfort with her led to my disclosing an interest in Ben and the deep feelings that were developing between us. I admitted to her that I was both excited and afraid. I had gambled and lost with Adam. The recovery period had been treacherous for my body and my soul. I didn't want the past to cast shadows on something fresh and new. Being able to talk to my mother about my new relationship was comforting. It served to further build the mother/daughter bond that had been abbreviated by time and circumstances.

After much contemplation, I decided to introduce my mother to Ben. It would be one more in the line of firsts for us. Usually I would have shared my news with Big Mama. Since she passed and my mother was back in my life, the new relational dynamic was welcomed and appreciated. I was beginning to value her opinion and, in my mind, she would be as enamored with him as I was. I deemed their introduction as just a formality. It would further validate my instincts about how right Ben and I were for each other. He could be the one.

My mother arrived for the dinner early and helped me prepare the meal for our special occasion. Being in the same kitchen cooking together reminded me of my youth and the joy we experienced as a normal nuclear family. Big Mama taught me well. The aroma that escaped from the food caused my mother to compliment me on my culinary skills. As we worked together, she probed deeper into the origins of my new relationship. At one point, I shook my head in amazement when I heard her voice repeat Big Mama's usual litany of questions. I just smiled and enjoyed the moment as the fruits of a typical parental exchange.

When the doorbell rang, the butterflies in my stomach all took flight at once in anticipation of my mother's reaction to meeting my new beau. Ben did not disappoint. There were kisses for me, flowers for the both of us and a bottle of wine for dinner. While I put the final touches on the meal, Ben and my mother began to get acquainted. Initially, the mood between the two of them was light, but it changed. From the kitchen, I heard portions of their conversation. I could have sworn I heard Big Mama's voice and intent. He was being examined like the grasshoppers we caught and put in jars during the summers at Big Mama's house. My mother asked questions that seemed a bit too personal for the occasion. If she was trying to make things awkward for him, she succeeded. Relief washed over his face when I announced dinner was served.

Much to my chagrin, the grilling didn't stop when the meal was served. Eventually, all the joy evaporated from the room as quickly as the heat abandoned our meal. All the probing questions and her suspicious demeanor made me think we were in the middle of a Columbo episode. After the relentless detective work continued, I couldn't decide what I wanted to do most; kick her under the table or crawl under the table. My mother wanted to know about his family, his friends, his last relationship, his best friend, and whether or not he owned his own home. I hadn't even asked Ben some of those things and we were dating. I could read his body language and he had been quite uncomfortable most of the evening. But through it all, he kept a smile on his face and endured. Relief washed over his face when he said his good-byes. I mouthed to him "I'm sorry" after he kissed me good night.

When I closed the door and turned around, my expression changed. Resentment was evident on my face. After preparing such a savory meal, I could not believe the highlight of the evening had been her expression of doubts about Ben. I was forced to sit silently and endure her insults over dinner, but I refused to stay quiet any longer. All the pent up anger I had choked down for far too many years breached my soul. It rushed forward with unrealized intentions. It brought with it all the frustrations, disappointments, hatred and fears that had festered inside for what seemed like an eternity.

"What makes you think you've earned the right to criticize me or any choices I've made? You abandoned me at Big Mama's. When you left, you took those rights with you. I'm a grown woman now. I don't need your approval or your comments about any decision I make."

Even though my voice had been elevated, my mother's voice was calm. "Prison taught me how to read people. This one didn't feel right to me. There's something artificial about him. I've seen his kind before. He's trouble."

"What are you talking about? He's not artificial, he's real. Why can't you just be happy for me? After everything I've been through, don't you think I am entitled to some happiness? Why are you trying to ruin this for me?"

"How much do you really know about him? Have you met his friends? His family? Been to his workplace? Been to his home? Ridden in his car?"

I had to admit I couldn't answer most of those questions in the affirmative.

"You shouldn't trust him as far as you can throw him. Slow down daughter. Take your time before you get too deep with this man. You may live to regret it."

"So you want to give me advice about men now. Like you have a good track record. Look at what you let happen to me with the last one you picked."

I surprised myself when I realized what I said. Those words had been stuck in my throat for years and now that they had been verbalized, they couldn't be taken back. The universe had captured their sound and had tucked them away in both of our minds until the opportunity to inflict their hurt again presented itself.

She stood quietly and patiently through my cathartic tirade. Her expression never changed. I had wanted to say those words for a long time. Now that they were all out, she finally knew how I felt. I was prepared for her futile attempt to deflect her role in the mess that crippled my life. But there was nothing but silence. She continued to look at me with eyes filled with guilt and pain. Her defeated eyes reminded me of the hollowness that existed when my father passed and she became an empty shell of a woman. I couldn't tell if the pain I observed was about our past or our future.

"Thank you daughter for giving me my freedom," was all she said before she turned and exited my apartment.

What had I done, and furthermore, was it worth it? I asked myself those questions as I sat there in the new apartment exhibiting old behavior. Just like Big Mama, her motives were to protect me, but I didn't appreciate her efforts. I refused to allow her to insult my decision about a man. I unburdened my soul by trampling on hers. What was wrong with me? I had not been the only one who had suffered. She had offered her freedom for mine, without the requirement of reciprocation. I couldn't imagine the degradation and humiliation she endured in a place where she had not belonged, just for me. We both had been injured by that experience and it would be impossible to tell whose wound had been the deepest. I was so confused by my actions and her response.

I had unmercifully lashed out at her a short time ago and I quickly regretted my actions. I couldn't let the next day begin without talking to my mother. I learned that lesson well with the passing of Big Mama and had became a great student of the instructor called life. The pop quizzes could be brutal. There were no re-tests or assignments graded on a curve and no one ever got to skip the final exams. The wiser version of me waited until I thought she was home and called her. We both apologized for how the evening ended and promised to get together again soon. Maybe by then, I would be able to show her how wrong her assessment had been about Ben.

FORTY

Back in Love Again

Ben planned a special night and I was anxious to be surprised. He stopped by the office earlier in the day and expressed a desire to plan an unforgettable evening for us. He arrived with a big smile and an even bigger bouquet of flowers, neither of which would be easily forgotten. Envy abounded in my workplace when I handed over my spare key. For the rest of the day, I found it hard to concentrate on work. The anticipation kept me distracted.

Walking through the door of my apartment was like stepping through a portal into the middle of a living fairy tale. The room was filled with too many flowers to count and their aroma was fresh and alluring to the senses. The trail of detached petals scattered throughout reminded me of spring blossoms that had fallen victim to gentle breezes. The endless amounts of flickering candles and the absence of ambient light produced a glowing effect throughout the room. The mood was further set by music that needed no words. Our harmony and cadence helped block out everything except the two of us. With all the beauty that had been created for this specific moment, the most beautiful thing in the room was Ben.

I could not have planned a more romantic rendezvous. For the entire evening, I was pampered to the nth degree. Everything was perfect; the food, the wine, the ambience and my companion. I knew I was being willingly seduced and loved every minute of the game. The evening was capped by the physical consummation of our bond. It fit seamlessly into the natural progression of our relationship. I hadn't been in the company of a man for a while and it became apparent I was hungry for some affection. I was comfortable with Ben and wanted to give my total self to him. Without hesitation, I took off my reserved façade and became the passionate person I had learned to express with Adam. Our skin melted together as our bodies shared common secrets and eliminated pent-up desires. Neither of us was disappointed with the outcome.

As much as we both wanted our time together to continue, the weekend ended. We were forced to face the conclusion of our enchanted encounter. As I reflected on the events of the past few days, I was encouraged by the possibility of this evolving into something special. I considered myself fortunate to have been selected by this man. Maybe I could be the one to entice him to take a desk job.

FORTY-ONE

Trouble in Paradise

The next few months were amazing. I enjoyed where this relationship train was headed and I had no intention of getting off any time soon. When Ben was not on a business trip, he spent the bulk of his time at my house. I was thrilled each time I came home and he was there. He always soothed away the rough edges of the day and made me feel special. I enjoyed that. I missed what it felt like to be part of a couple. When the weekend was over, I yearned to spend more time with him.

Knowing that he had a work trip planned provided the perfect opportunity for us to spend more quality time together. He could work all day and we could play at night. When I mentioned my idea to him, he rejected my suggestion.

He insulted me when he said, "Why would I ever do something like that? Didn't I tell you this was a work trip?"

"Yes, but you won't be working every hour of every day. I'm sure you get time off." I pushed my body up against his and cooed, "I'll be lonely while you're away."

Ben maintained the closeness of our bodies and caressed my back. His tone never changed when he replied, "I have clients to entertain and it is essential I make a good impression. What would I look like bringing you?"

Those words were unexpected. I waited for the punch line and the laughter at the end of the pregnant pause, but there was nothing. The silence confirmed the finality of his remarks. I couldn't believe his coldness. As much as I invited him to my work-related activities and into my social circle, he seemed uninterested in doing the same. I was confused.

Not many more words were spoken between us before it was time for bed. I remained on the couch until the snoring indicated I wouldn't have to face him again that night. I would not have to show the embarrassment I felt from possibly over-estimating the significance of this relationship. I was glad he would leave again tomorrow. I needed time to think without being distracted by his presence.

For the next few nights I was restless. I lay awake and questioned if we were both headed in the same direction. I didn't understand the motives behind Ben's words. I thought they were unkind. I was humiliated. I feared my eagerness for love may have outpaced my common sense. Even when he called, our exchanges were not as they once were. They felt forced and habitual. Although I wanted to chalk it up to the normal ebb and flow of a new relationship, I sensed something more profound was taking place. I questioned if I had moved too fast. I didn't want to consider that my mother's words may have been prophetic. Big Daddy once associated Adam and his family with dead flies. Different family, more flies.

Things didn't get better when he arrived at my apartment that weekend. The divide that existed between us advanced gradually, like a crack in the windshield. It started slowly but raced toward its full potential right in front of my eyes. I watched intently, but was powerless to impede its progress. We talked and even laughed about meaningless quips and news items, but avoided the elephant in the room.

Even the bedroom was under duress because of our differences. Unity and togetherness had become distant cousins as we lay there together, yet apart. The coldness of the physical and mental distance between us prevented our connection, even though I could feel the heat emanating from him. I wanted so badly to reach out and connect with any part of his body as confirmation of what we shared. I needed his touch to soothe my aching places and to possibly resuscitate our relationship. I struggled to remain calm and convey some semblance of control. As if he sensed my cravings, Ben shifted his body further away from me and buried himself deeper into the covers. Each unreciprocated acknowledgment of my presence brought another crack in my resolve. Defeated, I spent the night agitated and confused about the person on the other side of the bed. He was so different from the man I allowed to enter into my life a few short months ago.

FORTY-TWO

Speechless

B en never explained why he had harshly refused my
idea of combining work with a mini-vacation. My
goal was to extract that information in a non-confrontation-
al manner. I thought about the limited things we'd done
and the places we'd been. I wondered why I was not good
enough to be associated with him outside the local boundaries of this county. It felt like he was hiding me from his
friends and family. I needed answers and I was hell bent
on getting them when he returned from picking up dinner.

The anticipation of our impending conversation filled
me with mixed emotions. I had learned from previous lessons how the things that were swept under the rug often
tripped you up. Because we were in the early stages of this
relationship, there was no point of reference for the conflict
resolution skills of my partner. I didn't know when the proverbial line had been crossed or when I had ventured too far
into dangerous territory.

Our conversation started calmly and escalated quickly
as insults and accusations were hurled at each other from
places of hurt and confusion. I was in the middle of an ex-
pletive-filled rant fueled by disappointment and outrage,
when sound followed fury. The intense demonstration of

anger that erupted from his hands spilled over to my face with precision and purpose. The sound that pierced the room reminded me of a high-pitched firecracker. The force of his actions caused my balance to betray me. The remaining words in my mouth retreated and each letter assumed the natural position in the alphabet. None wanted to be close enough to each other to convey a legitimate thought. They had no desire to follow the aborted path of the first few words that had been swallowed up during the initial slap. I had to literally eat my own words and pretend the meal was satisfying. Their only hope of freedom would have been through regurgitation. They stayed put.

Somewhere in the midst of the commotion, he declared I had brought all this on myself. I was too aggressive and disrespectful and no one was allowed to talk to him like that. While I recoiled in disbelief, his face never registered anything other than normality. He didn't seem bothered by the trickle of blood that wandered from my nose or the leftover outline of his handprint that masqueraded as blush on the side of my face. With all the dignity I could muster, I steadied myself and gingerly walked toward the bathroom, assisted by the random pieces of furniture I encountered along the way.

I stood in the bathroom and looked in the mirror at my battered face. I saw the reflection of a person I swore years ago I would never be again, a victim. Yet there I stood with both my body and my ego bruised, trying to figure out what went wrong. I had become a member of the group of women I once categorized as pathetic and weak fools. It appeared I had assumed the same identity by default. Ben's actions were my initiation into the club.

My intellectual reasoning skills were no match for my current reality. No man had ever put his hands on me in anger. I didn't know how to manage my emotions after such an abrupt end to our discussion. I was an innocent battered woman. I was not delusional. I was not uneducated. I was not in poverty. I was falling in love, but I didn't deserve to be assaulted. I wasn't sure how his actions would change me. I asked myself what woman in her right mind allowed a man to beat on her and he not wake up with parts of himself missing the next day. Maybe I was about to find out since it was not beyond the realm of possibility for me to respond in that manner. After all, I was my mother's daughter. We both had a thing for knives.

The door slammed hard behind him and I flinched at the sharpness of that sound contrasted against the violating sound from moments ago. I was relieved I didn't have to look at Ben's face any time soon. I didn't want him to see the weakness and shame that polluted my eyes. Both my ego and my face were bruised. Time and space were required for me to figure out if I wanted to invest any more of my time in Ben. He displayed a frightening portion of himself that I vowed to never experience again. He called a couple of days later, but I wasn't ready to talk to him. The extra layer of make-up I was forced to apply continued to remind me of his actions. I needed more time.

As much as I wanted to confide in my mother, I couldn't, especially after she had expressed her concerns about his character. I didn't want to face the "I told you so" look she would surely give me after the verbal tongue-lashing I blessed her with. I was forced to singularly carry this burden and find my own solution. I didn't want to acknowledge the possibility of my being alone again. Being alone would represent another example of my failure as a woman. I had never been able to carry a baby to term and I couldn't keep a man. What element of substance did I have to offer the world as a contributing member of the female population?

I felt so unbalanced. I was standing on the shore of my own life watching the sands shift uncontrollably beneath me. I had not seen or spoken to Ben in weeks and I wondered if I would welcome his presence again. I used that time to decide whether or not he was the man for me. Each night that I didn't hear from him made me lean further toward the "not". Nevertheless, I still watched the door like a lovesick puppy waiting on its master to come home. Each night I pretended to be engrossed in the chatter from the television and often fell asleep on the sofa. I spent too many ordinary nights alone. I didn't want to admit how much I missed having Ben around. I didn't condone his actions, but was determined not to send the wrong message. Eventually, I would be forced to make a decision and it had to be sooner, rather than later.

A hot bath had been just what I needed. I appreciated the relaxation that always accompanied one of my favorite childhood rituals. I drifted off to sleep with the television serving as my companion. The shadows it cast gave the appearance of movement on the other side of the bed. For a moment I thought my desires were playing tricks on me as the familiar smell of Ben's cologne invaded my senses. I felt the covers move and his body sliding close to mine with familiarity. His hands and arms made contact with my body and his skilled touch lured me into him. "Baby I'm so sorry" was the hook and he reeled me in with heartfelt confessions of regret. The soothing words in my ear washed away any thoughts of terminating our relationship. I knew in my heart that he was sorry; I just needed to hear him say it.

Our connection that night was unlike anything I had experienced with him before. We remained engulfed in the splendor of our reunion for hours. We lay there cuddled in contentment and inhaled the aroma of our union. The violent events of the past quickly faded from my memory. I knew without a doubt the man laying here with me now could have never meant to hurt me. We forgave each other for the misunderstanding and vowed to only lay loving hands on each other. The spiritual and physical reconciliation was the elixir we used to get back on track. After that night, our connection would be stronger than ever. Maybe Ben was right. I could have been too demanding and aggressive because I was feeling insecure. He had just shown me how much he cared for me and that was all that really mattered.

The return to normalcy occurred quicker than I anticipated as we fell back into a comfortable routine. We enjoyed each other more frequently and passionately than ever before. We never wanted to be away from each other. It felt like we had known each other for years, even though I had met him only a few months ago. If this was any indication of what was to come, I was so glad I took Big Mama's advice about finding love again. I wanted what my daddy and mother had. I was certain I had found that rare connection with Ben. He appeared to be the answer to my dreams.

FORTY-THREE

True Blue

I knew immediately what that feeling was, but for weeks I had been too afraid to express it to the universe. The thin blue colored line was striking against the vast white surface. I was filled with a joy that could no longer be suppressed. I gently rubbed my mid-section in anticipation of what was to come. I would have another chance to be a mother. Finally, I would know what it would be like to have someone love me just because. That's what I missed out on with the interruption of my last maternal experience. It would feel good to be wanted, not just for my looks or the curves bestowed on me by Mother Nature or the coveted crevices that became the obsession of the male species, but just for me. All the love that I would have for them would be more than enough. I would be beautiful to them and needed by them and oh how I would love my little bundle of joy. I would finally be complete and would have what I wanted for a long time; a family.

I had often wondered if this day would ever come again and questioned myself as a woman. All life forms have the capacity to reproduce, but not me. Why couldn't I do it? It was the most natural thing in the world for the female species. People are considered the highest form of being, oth-

187

er than the Almighty, but my performance in this area had been inferior to that of mere animals. It really didn't take much effort and I clearly understood the biology of the act. I questioned why my womb was treated like the children of Israel during the original Passover. I hadn't had trouble conceiving. My challenge had been with maintaining the pregnancy. Without a child, I considered myself a failure as a woman.

For the better part of my life my mind told me that my first maternal experience didn't count. I had grown weary of being less than honest about the number of pregnancies I experienced with zero live births recorded. I always subtracted one. The nature of its origin had been too painful and I disavowed its existence. I paid dearly for that experience. The midwife had been ill equipped to provide the post traumatic care my barely pubescent womb required. Consequently, the lack of proper care contributed to my inability to carry a baby to term. But all of that was about to change. I knew nothing in life was certain, but I really felt this pregnancy would be a success. This would not be like the other time that ended in disappointment and grief when I was informed that the insensitive natural selection process had claimed my joy. I didn't know how many more chances I would get at motherhood. Three had to be my magic number for this victory.

Those frustrations had been part of my past and now I was looking forward to a future with my new man. We had shared many details about our past, but he knew nothing about the unyielding psychological struggles I concealed related to completing the woman-identifying task of giving birth. Most external scars show the manifestation of the healing process. It's the internal ones that take the longest time to heal and seem to never fade away. I had been scarred for life. The only way I could escape the disappointments associated with my past was to start fresh and see where these new beginnings would lead.

Having voiced similar opinions and desires about having a family, I was confident Ben would be as excited as I was about our possibilities. Big Mama said I should live again and that is exactly what I intended to do. I had moved on, not just figuratively, but physically. I was filled with hope and the positive energy that came along with loving life again. Adding the new baby would make me complete. I would have what my mother and daddy had and we would be just as happy as they were. All I had ever wanted was my family back and if I couldn't have it one way, I would have it another.

The night of my big announcement arrived and I couldn't wait to share the good news. I had been holding in my secret for over a month. I thought I would explode if I didn't tell him about the product of our union. I felt like the child who had peeked at the Christmas presents and had to conceal the deception until the gifts were finally opened. Because something of this magnitude deserved special treatment, I had planned a night as special as the one he had created for me. Everything related to this celebration of new beginnings had to be perfect.

When he first arrived and noticed a meal consisting of his favorite foods was being prepared, he couldn't conceal his appreciation for my efforts. After looking around the room, as if he were searching for something, he asked if my mother was there too. We both laughed and shared a moment of lightness. We settled into the ritualistic exercise of filling in the gaps of time since we were last together as I put the finishing touches on our meal. Throughout the evening, I was bubbling with excitement and couldn't wait to behold his reaction to the announcement of our hopes and my dreams. I was anxious for the preliminary portion of the night to be over so that we could move to the true purpose of my extra special treatment. The night had been filled with all his favorite things. I hoped my announcement would be the item he cherished the most.

When the word pregnant tumbled from my lips, the color drained from his face, his eyes became the size of saucers, and the prolonged coughing nearly warranted the Heimlich maneuver. After gaining his composure his body language suggested displeasure with my revelation. He fought to find the right words to convey the thoughts that quickly cycled through his mind. He became closed off and protective of his true feelings. The emotional distance staked its claim in the center of our conversation. The scenario I conjured up in my mind did not mirror the outcome. My joy became his pain.

FORTY-FOUR

Ultimatum

The news of our bundle had not contained the joy I anticipated. Ben spoke his disappointment in disgust and asked, "How could you have done something as stupid as getting pregnant? What's wrong with you?" He nervously paced the floor wringing his hands, and then he said, "How hard is it to avoid a pregnancy? It's as simple as taking a pill. How could you screw that up?"

He didn't hesitate before he delivered the most heartless statement of all.

"If you are thinking of keeping this baby, you will not have my support. Right now, you need to let me know when you are going to take care of this problem. If you keep it, you will lose me. It's that simple."

His words cut through me like hot lead. I must have heard something wrong because I knew Ben didn't just ask me to abandon my chance to complete a mission that had been impossible up until now. My decision had been made long before I met him. I didn't need him to approve any choices I made about my body. Any chance of fulfilling the longing that festered inside me would be given full access to the possibility of success. He was aware of my past challenges with motherhood and had expressed loving concern regarding my plight. Without question, he should have already known that ultimatum was pointless.

Ben continued to berate me about being pregnant. He reacted as if I ruined his life. I wasn't prepared for the harshness. I wanted one reaction, I got the opposite. After all, it was my baby too. My opinion had to count for something. Ben was very active and present for the conception, but he considered my familial status as my individual failure. He appeared unconcerned about my feelings. All that mattered was what he wanted. There was no "we", it was "him" and his needs, then "me" fulfilling his needs. I didn't see where my needs fit into his happiness equation.

Timidity replaced my once bold posture after being emotionally battered by the intermittent rants and his accusatory looks. Out of necessity, I withdrew, as I once did, into my protective cocoon. The absence of his desire for a child and my misinterpretation of his familial aspirations settled into my spirit. All I could do was apologize for disappointing him as I fought the sadness that crept into my heart. My tears could no longer be contained as I began to understand the enormity of my pending decision. But those tears meant nothing to him. He left me standing in the hallway weeping and confused. He announced that I wasn't the woman he thought I was and he needed time to think. I needed time to think, too. I wanted the time and space to figure out how a night that was meant to be so special ended up being an emotional catastrophe.

Things didn't look better when morning overtook

night. I lay there still distressed about Ben's reaction to our pregnancy. I spent a restless night searching for answers. I couldn't understand why he wasn't the least bit accepting of this pregnancy. After the initial shock of the announcement wore off, I was confident he would come around to the idea of being a father. Calm would replace anxiety and eventually, he would be happy about this gift. Why wouldn't he be? He said he wanted kids. Now that it was within reach, he was undermining at our happiness. What had I missed?

Maybe the stress and the sudden change to our relationship caused him to balk at the news. The first time I made this same announcement to an unprepared father, his reaction had been one of disbelief as well. Eventually, Adam warmed up to the expectant father role and celebrated our creation. After he got use to the idea of being a father, I was certain Ben's attitude would change. But what if acceptance never came? What then? Did he truly understand the sacrifice he was asking me to make?

I didn't know how I would be able to live with myself if I heeded his desires. I would lose more than he could begin to comprehend if I did what he asked. At that juncture in my life, I needed a win in the baby column. I didn't have the strength or mental fortitude to withstand another loss. This time, I had to put myself first. He would have to decide if he wanted to continue with me on my journey to motherhood. That was the only path I was ready and willing to take. If he wanted to go in the opposite direction, I would not impede his path, but he would not dictate mine.

FORTY-FIVE

Mother Knows Best

I was still reeling from Ben's ultimatum. The more my mind lingered on the subject of my pregnancy, the more I desired guidance about my impending decisions. I never imagined such diametrically opposed stances would exist between two people who had professed similar desires. Normally, things of such magnitude were discussed with Big Mama, but she was in heaven. I had to lean on my mother for the necessary love and support. We had made so much progress rebuilding our relationship and I needed to talk to someone who would understand my desperate need to have a family. Since coming back into each other's lives, we had gotten more comfortable with our relationship as adults and I was beginning to trust her again.

My mother was happy to hear from me and we agreed to meet for lunch later that day. True to our words, we had not let the frustrations expressed during the previous culinary event tear down what we had built up. But in all honesty, those words, even though they were harsh, needed to be spoken so the slate of my anger could be wiped clean. We both understood that freeing my suppressed resentment was the only way we could continue to move forward.

Notwithstanding her feelings about my romantic choice,

our severed bond was being restored. We both were enjoying the structured reclamation process. I was anxious to talk to my mother about my challenges. However, I was unsettled about the amount of information I would share about my new relationship. I didn't want to hear the disappointment in her voice or see the pain in her eyes. After Ben assaulted me, I avoided face-to-face contact with my mother until all physical evidence of his battering had faded away. It would not have been worth the risk to any of us to disclose information about a problem that had already been resolved. The last time someone harmed me physically, her actions toward him were unmerciful. I couldn't fathom the additional skills she had picked up during her years of incarceration. I would hate for her to go away again because of me.

This new dilemma I faced could not be remedied by the simple passage of time. Unlike the handprint that had lingered on my face, a protruding belly could not be covered up with make-up or explained away as an inadvertent connection with the proverbial door. No matter what decision I made, the residual effects would continue to have an impact on many lives. Ben's obligatory solution was unacceptable. If he wanted a way out, it was there. I would be more than willing to allow him to walk away, but I could not abandon this gift.

Although I was steadfast about my decision, I wanted to seek advice and validation from my mother about the weighty consequences I faced. I was nervous about disclosing my impending status change. It would drastically change both of our lives. I wondered how she would react when I gave her the news that I would be a mother and she would be a grandmother. Even though she did not like the mate I had chosen, I hoped she would understand my decision to move forward with the pregnancy, with or without Ben's support.

The love and understanding that she showed me during my revelation was what I needed most. The squeals of joy reminded me of my youthful days when the secrets I shared with my childhood friends were stowed away from the world. I had to reign her in as she started making plans for a baby shower and recommending names. Her excitement had been what I so desperately desired from Ben. The loving embrace and genuine bliss warmed my heart and lifted my spirits. No judgement, just a mother's love. I felt it, and it felt so good.

For a moment, I felt like the small child she comforted thru the sadness and confusion that took root in our lives after my father passed. In her arms, I felt at home as the years filled with hurts, anger and misconceptions thawed in her embrace. She was still the mother I needed her to be. I was happy she was in my life again. Thank God for Big Mama, who became the placeholder for my mother until we were able to find each other again. She kept my heart intact and ready for our reunion, regardless of how hard I fought against her. I don't know where in the world I would have been without both of those women being so prominent in my life.

FORTY-SIX

Bridges

After returning home from our outing, I was truly happy about the way my life was taking shape. My mother was happy for me and that pleased me more than I had expected. She had validated my concerns and stood firmly behind my decision. I was still the little girl who wanted to make her mother proud. She had commended me on my strength of character and true dedication to my parental desires.

Each time we were together and I gained insight from her perspective about our time apart, I admired her more. I marveled at her ability to survive those years when the gaps created by distance and time were exploited. On one visit, she showed me faded articles and photos from times I had forgotten, but had brought joy to her soul during her incarceration. She felt she could have endured anything as long as she knew I was no longer in danger. Among those photos were the ones we took at the photo booth. During my youth, I had considered those photos some of my most prized possessions. I often wondered how they had escaped from my treasure chest. The photos showed how happy and connected we had been that day. At that time, we had been recovering from a long separation and they represented the release of relational stress and forward movement toward normalcy. The irony of this moment could not be overlooked. We made plans to find a photo booth to memorialize the parallel stages of our lives.

To my surprise, she showed me pictures and programs from both of my graduations. Her face and posture showed nothing but pride as she spoke of how she witnessed my accomplishing a milestone that she and my father had desired for me. She had sat through the commencement ceremonies and cried tears of sorrow for not being able to congratulate me in person. I realized that even though I had rejected her, she had been content to exist in the shadows of my life until I was ready to forgive her. It was overwhelming to realize how much she had continued to sacrifice for me.

I noticed my mother staring intently at my neck and out of curiosity, asked if something was wrong. I was wearing a necklace that Big Mama had given me. Since she passed, it had become one of my most prized possessions. She had not given me full custody of this trinket until I was eighteen. She feared that my irresponsible actions would result in an inadvertent windfall for someone else. Big Mama had called it a family heirloom and had told me to cherish the family members who had provided such a history-filled gift for me.

It shocked me when my mother described the inscription on the back side of the locket and proceeded to tell me the history surrounding my gift. My mother had given this locket to my Big Mama before she had gone to prison. In my youth, Big Mama had only allowed it to be worn on special occasions. I did not realize that each time I had proudly worn it, I had carried around a piece of my mother with me. She had been just a jewelry chest away during some of the best and worst times of my life. She had been with me, even during those times when I doubted the depth of her love.

Becasue our minds are vast and limitless, we often manipulate our gift. We sometimes distort the truth in an effort to protect our sanity and control the actions of others. In the absence of concrete facts, I had conjured up my own truth, even if it had not been accurate. I believed everything I had told myself. My focus had been on my own survival. I did what was necessary for survival. Because we are emotional creatures, we are often lead astray by the tricks of our mind. We go in search of half-truths and archaic discoveries that can lead to closure for some or the opening of old wounds for others. My life had taken a self-preservation detour. It was critical that I change directions, now that I had discovered more facts. My mis-truths about my mother's motives had comforted me in bad times, betrayed me in good times and kept me bound most of the time. Freedom felt good.

FORTY-SEVEN

Too Late

The impending doctor's appointment had me on edge. The night before the visit was filled with much trepidation. I had flashbacks of my last clinical visit and I trembled at the thought of another defeat at the hands of nature. Fear taunted me and I knew I could not attend the appointment alone. Although Ben wasn't interested in accompanying me, my mother was overjoyed. There was no way she would squander the opportunity to hear her grandchild's heartbeat. Those memories were meant to be shared by loved ones.

It took about an hour to make it official. The tests confirmed that for the last twenty-two weeks, my body had housed my long awaited dream. That was the longest I had carried a child. It was a good sign. For now, everything was going well and the baby's heartbeat was strong. Maybe this time my womb would be capable enough to bear the weight of my deferred dreams of motherhood. We were all smiles when we left the appointment. The official pregnancy pronouncement brought confirmation that my decision to ignore his wishes was the right choice.

In contrast, I could not quite get a read on Ben's true feelings. His mood and his motives vacillated from one extreme to the next. One minute he appeared settled with the idea of fatherhood; other times he was angry. He could be very gentle and supportive when he tried to coax me into agreeing to his termination proposal. Other times he was aggressive and demanded that I take care of our problem immediately. At times, when he thought I wasn't looking, I believed I detected evil behind his looks of contempt for my transforming exterior.

I hoped he would have been more accepting, but that was not the case. I found it odd that he never touched my stomach or asked any questions about how the pregnancy was progressing. There were no hugs from behind that encompassed both of us; no smiles or expressed dreams about having a son or a daughter and no introduction of himself to his first child. Some part of me still hoped we had a chance at happiness, but the more time that passed, the more I could see the end of this relationship rapidly approaching. I wasn't a naive teen anymore. My time with Adam taught me that this type of relational crisis signaled an impassable roadblock. Usually, no temporary detours would keep the relationship moving forward.

Ben started making his presence scarce. Part of me believed his absence was more about my pregnancy and less about work. But I was fine with the separation. I used that time to think about me and what I wanted and the possibility of single motherhood. At the conclusion of all my pondering, my response was "so what". My decision would not be an anomaly. Millions of capable women have navigated these same familial waters without regard to the underlying circumstances. Ben would be back from his business trip next week. There would have to be a meeting of minds that were moving in opposite directions. I was sure his first question would be about the outcome of his petition for me to choose between the baby and our relationship. My mind had not changed about maintaining my pregnancy. He left a note and enough money to complete the "procedure". He promised to take me somewhere special once I healed. I guess we wouldn't be taking a trip any time soon. I was sure he hadn't realized that during his extended absence, the possibility of exercising the termination option became a medical impossibility.

I was not looking forward to our exchange of information related to the status of my pregnancy. After I revealed how far along I was and that this matter could not be easily "taken care of", he became totally closed off. His body was there, but his mind was elsewhere. After the last conversation, I realized things were not progressing in the right direction. I reconciled myself to the fact that I may be in this alone. I was not afraid. I was strong enough and willing to let go of the dream man before more nightmares polluted my existence. I saw the looks he gave me. I feared the anger would eventually overcome any remaining good feelings that had been generated from our months of togetherness. I let Ben know that it would be better with him, but still good without him. In the end, he would have to make a choice. I already made mine. I decided to continue with the pregnancy. I was more than ready to stand firm on my decision.

FORTY-EIGHT

Tripped Up

Ben's business trip lasted longer than normal and I couldn't control the urge to call him. I wanted to talk through our differences while we were apart. I hoped he had changed his attitude about my pregnancy. We talked briefly and I reiterated that I wanted to keep our baby. I was prepared for the onslaught of negativity comparable to the words that accompanied the initial announcement. To my surprise, he appeared to accept the fact that I didn't, and now couldn't, end the pregnancy. He promised to be supportive of my decision. That was his response while we were on the phone. I didn't know what to expect upon his return.

Lately, there had been too much tension between us. During his visit, I wanted us to be normal again. We could allow our physical reunion to restore our bond. Each time we were apart for an extended period of time, it was intense when our bodies reintroduced themselves. We just needed to enjoy each other's company and use that as a way to close the distance between us. He would be here soon and I wanted our reunion to be free from the negative energy that crowded out our happiness.

Our reunion didn't go as planned. It had been nearly three weeks since we had been in each other's company. Nature's obligations caused my body to blossom with fullness and curvature as it marched cheerfully toward motherhood. The welcome embrace was cold and Ben appeared annoyed when my stomach made contact with him. He quickly moved backward. His movement signaled his continued unacceptance of my decision and set the tone for the remainder of the evening. I endured forced conversations and one syllable responses as his focus centered on anything but me. I began to wonder why he even bothered to come over. He appeared content to direct his attention to the artificial lives being lived out on a television screen rather than deal with the pressing issues of our lives. Before I became totally exasperated, I announced my plans for a shower, hoping that the hot water would be both physically and mentally refreshing.

After I turned on the shower, I realized how desperately I wanted to salvage the remainder of our evening. We had often enjoyed each other's company in the steamy shower and I longed for that type of connection again. This solution could be beneficial for both of us. I could put on some soothing music, light a scented candle and invite him into the shower where he would be welcome to partake of anything he could put his hands on.

His back was to me when I entered the room and I heard him talking to someone on the phone. The words I heard coming from his mouth rocked me to my core.

"No, I haven't forgotten about our anniversary. I'll be

home tomorrow night. Daddy loves you too, baby. Now can you put mommy on the phone?"

"Hey baby", was all my mind could absorb before my feet rebelled. They wouldn't move any closer to him. They acted as if they were stuck in cement. I audibly sucked in air before quickly putting my hand over my mouth so no sounds of anguish could escape. I began to reverse my steps and quietly removed myself from the room, not daring to take my eyes off him. I slowly retreated until his voice was no longer distinct and became no more than muffled sounds. Just a few more steps remained until I could be within the confines of my impromptu safe haven. Then, I would be able to exhale.

I was careful not to close the door with the force appropriate for my anger. It found the proper connection before I released the knob and allowed the mechanism to rest in the jamb. I stood there momentarily feeling as if I were in a mental coma. I kept trying to push the pause button on the infinite loop of words that would not stop playing in my mind. "Daddy", "Anniversary", "Baby". Who was he calling "Baby"? That was his term of endearment for me. My mind suddenly slowed down enough to encapsulate the true meaning of his spoken words. My internal voice kept uttering what my heart refused to accept, but what I knew to be true. That man was married and already had a wife and a child. He had completed my dreams with someone else. My dreams had been ambushed by reality. The life that we had spent months building was no more stable than the houses of those two little pigs that got blown away by the big bad wolf. I, too, had been blown away by my own married wolf in adultery-ready clothing.

Eventually, I released the door knob and engaged the lock. Unexpectedly, the clicking sound invited dormant emotions to rapidly force their way to the surface. Those emotions took me back to my youth and the feelings harbored by an innocent child who brutally became the victim of a sexual predator. I remembered when the bathroom had been the only safe place where I could express my true feelings after being assaulted. Once again, I was trapped between four small walls trying to make sense of things that were beyond my reasoning and control. In my youth, I had been physically assaulted; this time I had been mentally abused. The parallels between then and now could not be ignored. I thought I had moved far beyond the clutches of my past, yet there I was being confronted by quarantined memories and bitter thoughts.

Mirror, Mirror

R etreating into the bathroom with his secret had been
one of the hardest but most rational course of action.
I had not been sure how to responsibly react to what I had
just heard. Even though I could still hear the truth ringing
in my ears, I didn't want to acknowledge its significance. I
had invested too much of myself into this relationship for
it to just be the lie it turned out to be. I needed my version
of the truth to validate our union. But I was unable to find
an unblemished fact that would devalue his spoken words.
His audible truth, not my internal narrative, had prevailed.
It was time to acknowledge his facts and surrender.

It had been all I could do to keep from crying out in
pain while remaining in the solitary confinement of the
bathroom. My hurt and anger told me to confront his lies
and deception right then and let the chips fall where they
may. I had nothing to lose since he was not now, nor had
he ever been truly mine. I quickly decided that course of
action was irrational. It would liquidate the power of the
unexpected truth I struggled to conceal and contain within the bowels of my safe haven. I needed to remain calm
to somehow find logic in an illogical situation. I hoped the

hot shower would wash away some of the sting of the recent revelation. I stood quietly under the continual flow of the water. I allowed the constant stream to drown out the hurt with sounds I could control. But there was not enough water in the ocean, let alone the hot water tank, to calm my mind and soothe where I ached.

My tears flowed freely down my body as they carved out their escape route to the drain. My mind replayed our first time together and the beauty of our union. But those memories couldn't roost before the words and figures with no faces, wearing name tags that read "child" and "wife" crowded them out. They pushed my dreams into oblivion. They couldn't remain, given the exposure to the truth. The shower stall became my momentary support system and the gentle hand in my back that kept me from buckling under the weight of disappointment. The water eventually began to lose its warmth. I was forced to think about what awaited me at the end of my impossible attempt to remove the essence of Ben's touch from my pregnant body and my disorganized mind. I was not ready to accept defeat. I wanted hope to caress my protruding middle and tell me that all would be ok. I waited on it until the water turned cold. I was forced to exit the shower with only his truth.

Even after being physically cleansed, I still felt dirty. I began to comprehend the gravity of the situation that we both were facing. Someone other than me had been betrayed as well. It appeared there was a family to consider that wasn't mine. I had assumed a role in a tragedy I never auditioned for. I inadvertently became an accomplice in the violation of someone's sacred vows. Given the limited amount of available options that would leave someone in a non-envious position, I was concerned about what the future would hold. It was becoming painfully obvious that I would be the odd-man out.

The layers of conflict that surrounded me in the make-shift isolation chamber included my past, my present and my future. I stood pensively in front of the foggy mirror trying to compose myself before facing him again. Mirrors hold no bias. They are always forced to present the truth, no matter how we choose to filter the light. My soul had been stripped naked. I stared at the totally exposed being in the mirror. I momentarily entertained the internal dialogue that kept soliciting my skepticism in an attempt to mask the sadness within. I recalled the same feeling the night his handprint tattoo accented my face. In both cases, I knew the truth when I heard it and felt it. Looking at the spot on my face where he had imposed his will, the word fool appeared and began to flash like a neon light. The words desperate, gullible, needy, pathetic, blind, and finally, mistress, each took their time in the spotlight. They summarized the ugly side of our time together and emphasized how insignificant I had been. The initial battering incident should have been enough for me to cut all ties with Ben. That moment had been my way out, but I chose not to take it. I had contradicted my standards to conform to his and my selfish desires. Little did I know that doing so would have changed the direction of my life and ushered in consequences I never imagined were possible. I had been standing too close to the mirror to see the true reflection and direction of our relationship.

Despite how our things appeared before I entered the bathroom, the status quo could not remain upon my exit. There was no way that I could willingly lay down with a married man again. I was sure my skin would revolt the next time he touched me because of my aversion to infidelity. I had no duplicity in the betrayal of his marital commitment, but I felt distressed by my entanglement in their lives. I was so ashamed at how I had been so eager to give myself away, mind, body and good sense, to become a temporary physical distraction to that man for the price of a cup of coffee and a few meaningless gifts.

Uncertainty lurked beyond the confines of the bathroom door. I wondered how I would react when our eyes met again. Because I could not reveal this betrayal until I was ready, I had a role to play and I had to be convincing. In my script, the last twenty minutes never happened and I was still grateful Ben had returned from his business trip. I had to appear to still believe the lie that was staring me in my face and ringing in my ears. I took a deep breath, swallowed my resentment and prayed my face would not reveal my broken heart. To my relief, Ben was asleep. I didn't have to face him. I wouldn't share a bed with him ever again and I didn't have to explain why. I quietly made my way to the couch, unaware of the parts of my past that followed me down that corridor.

FIFTY

Rewind

The moment my body stretched out on the couch, I realized how emotionally exhausted I had become. I felt numb; as if I had been bathed in Orajel. The past saturated my mind with yesterday's pain and toyed with my emotions. The whirlwind of emotions merged my past thoughts with my current circumstances until I was caught up in a vortex of pain that surrounded me from every direction. I was both a child and adult whose story of exploitation had been essentially the same.

My first attacker silenced my objections with his hands. I covered my own mouth to prevent the sounds of pain caused by the mental attack from being heard. I once sat in a cauldron of hot water trying to cleanse my broken body. In contrast, I stood with my face toward the steady stream of water, hoping for a cleansing as well. I was still unable to control tears that escaped from my eyes and meandered down any part of my body they encountered. I was content to allow the water to dilute my tears, in an effort to release the pain. Once again, my abuser had the ability to lie in the bed of a willing woman, yet he chose to abuse me. A couch would once again be my default destination and my resting place after another assault. The contradiction that waited for me in that bedroom down the hall would never physically explore me again. But I would yet again have to recover from being abused by a man, with his gift to me being the bearing of maternal fruit produced by his seed.

Waking up made me realize I had fallen asleep, even though I felt as if the four hours since my last cognizant thought had not passed. My mind immediately cycled through the evening's events. I fought to bring calmness to my spirit. The past invaded the present. The two realms joined forces in the destruction of any internal peace I hoped would occur before the morning gifted me with yesterday's sorrow.

The overwhelming feeling of being assaulted caused me to react as if I were still in the moments following the destruction of my innocence. I began to think of all the things I should have done back then. I even blamed myself for portions of the disturbing outcome. If only I had told someone, if only I had defended myself harder or found a way to cry for help, my mother would have saved me. My entire life would have been different. My mother would have never spent those critical years away from me and he would have spent the time he had earned in jail. That had been a pivotal time in our lives. It bothered me that he never expressed regret for his actions and the pain it caused in our lives. It was apparent that the pain he inflicted on my innocent, virginal body was still viable. He had devalued me as a human being and I didn't know how to rid myself of the anger unearthed by a similar circumstance. My mother carried her rage for years, until she visited retribution on my attacker as a surrogate for the one she couldn't punish. I believe it had freed her from that dark time. No doubt, it healed returned portions of innocence for the small child whose carefree existence had been snatched away. The burden and shame she was forced to carry, on shoulders too weak to support such heavy life weights, was lifted. It would be the night I settled the same score. I was determined to punish the punisher.

I felt possessed as I made my way from the couch into the kitchen. The knife made a swooshing noise when I withdrew it from the block. The sounds echoed in my ear and encouraged me to avenge my honor. I wondered how my mother felt as she prepared to settle the score with my attacker. Did she envision my assault? Could she hear my tears screaming for help? Did her rage masquerade as courage as she made her way toward their bedroom? Was it the face of her own attacker she saw when his appendage, the source of his pride and the weapon of his abuse, lay lifeless and non-threatening in her hand? Did his screams validate her juvenile pain? Did she think of the consequences that would follow after the anger subsided? Whatever she felt, it was all justified. But I didn't have time to linger on those past decisions. It was time for me to take back my innocence.

The hallway beckoned me to move forward into my past. Beyond its end was his safe haven; the place where he stumbled to after depositing years of damage within my core. I began to re-trace his steps with conviction and purpose. I was stealthy in my approach, and mimicked the youthful quiet pilgrimage to eavesdrop on Big Mama's conversations.

I cautiously peeked into the room and heard the snoring sounds that accompanied his respite from the cares of the world. He lay there in comfort, not knowing how his cowardice had impacted my life. I became irritated that he could lay there as if nothing abnormal happened. He displayed no shame; no remorse. My anger continued to build. I became fixated on exactly how and where to focus my efforts.

My mental map of the room allowed me to quietly make my way to the bed without turning on the light. I stood over him, in turmoil, as he lay peacefully sleeping. With each elongated blink, the face on the pillow changed from the past to the present abuser. My emotions wandered between each realm. The bundled rage continued to creep up my spine and through my eyes; eyes which in that moment saw the face of my discontent. I needed to settle the score with him and to take back my power. It would be so easy to attack him as deceitfully as he had attacked me for his distasteful pleasure. It would be so easy to just slide under the covers and entice the serpent to make an appearance before making him pay for his sins. It would be my chance to conquer his mind and body as violently as mine had been. I needed to see him writhing in pain. The expression of anguish would be audible retribution for his past wrongs. Somewhere from within, a voice kept shouting at me to use my rage to exact my revenge. "Now, do it now. Punish him for your hurt; punish him for your pain. Give him what he deserves. Now, do it now!"

With the knife firmly in my hand, I leaned over the bed and moved back the covers in search of his weapon. Without warning, the baby violently moved against my insides. It caused me to wince in pain. I fell to my knees beside the bed, dropped the knife to the floor and began to rub my stomach. My baby's voice never reached the atmosphere, but I heard its plea. It reminded me that both of us would lose if I exacted revenge. I would become no better than the ones I despised. The loudspeaker in my head paused long enough to interrupt the corrupt instructions that were playing in my mind. The silence allowed me to redirect my focus toward the future, not the noise of my past. Because I had found my own peace, I allowed my tormentor's sleep to continue. Karma would find its way to his world without my help.

With the help of my unborn child, I found my moment of clarity. I realized I was better than those who sought to destroy me. No matter whose face was on the pillow at the moment of my attack, my child and I would also end up being punished. I had served every day of my mother's imprisonment with her. I didn't want to sentence my child to the same. There were many things about my nights of sorrow that were comparable, but losing the ability to be with my child would not be one of them. I had no right to vengeance; I only had the right to the truth I already knew. Nothing could be gained when compared to what I would lose. If I had carried out my revenge, I would have aborted my chance at finally being a mother. My family's legacy of maternal regret had to end with me. The only appendage that needed to be separated from Ben's body was me. I had to take back my power differently than my mother; not with anger, but with courage. I realized how close I had come to disaster. It scared me.

My freedom and my happiness were up to me. I had to stop giving someone else dominion over my life. I required nothing more from either of the men who temporarily caused the disruption of my life's path. They would have no more power over me than I was willing to concede. I became inspired by the self-determination that replaced the confusion in my mind and the knife in my hand. I was ready to let go of everything that tied me to those men, except my child. In order for my own healing to begin, I had to separate myself and my child from the aura of abuse and deception. In less than twenty-four hours, more chaos would be expelled from my life.

FIFTY-ONE

Baggage

The morning welcomed me with the sound of his stir-
ring in the next room. Even though my sleep had
been interrupted by an excursion into dark places, I felt
refreshed. The decision to exit the bedroom and close the
door on things I couldn't change was sound. I had allowed
the spirit and the truth of restoration to inhabit my place
of comfort and peace. After last night's revelation and my
courtship with vengeance, I recognized how drastic the
changes in my life had to be. I felt like a rubber band that
had been stretched too far, too long. The tension may have
gone away, but I would never be in the same shape before
those pressure filled moments. I would try, but I was not
sure when I would be able to snap back.

As much as I wanted to confront him, I knew I wasn't
ready. Until last night, most things had been done on Ben's
terms. This time they would be on mine. But first, I needed
to rid myself of a mind full of unhealthy thoughts before I
could have a rational conversation with the poser. He had
posed as a single man, but he was clearly married. Hours
ago, I overheard his plans to celebrate another wedding anniversary. He had posed as someone who longed for chil-

dren, but tried to turn me into the killer of my own dreams in order to protect his lies. He already had a child. He posed as someone with whom I could build a future, but there was no future for us. I would soon be his past. My recent discovery represented a betrayal of my intimacy. It tore down parts of the self-esteem wall I spent years rebuilding. I allowed him to get close enough to infect my heart with hope, only to have it ripped out of my chest. I would be forever changed by those events.

I heard him talking in the other room before I felt him standing over me. I continued to lay motionless on the sofa. I pretended to be asleep. I mastered that game in my youth. My arm was positioned over my face so I could view his movements undetected. He lingered momentarily in the kitchen before I heard him leave. The note on the counter explained he went out for breakfast and didn't want to wake me. I estimated I had about twenty minutes before his return. During that time, I gathered his belongings and mentally prepared myself for the confrontation that could not be avoided.

After all of his things were out of my bedroom, I sat silently on the sofa awaiting his return. My mind would not stay still and went searching for the unknown. My world had been saturated with lies and fantasies. I wasn't sure where deception ended and truth began. There was so much more about that man that I didn't know. I began to question every action and nuance of our relationship. Who was he? What about him was real? Was I the business trip excuse for his family? Was I some game that had gone overtime with the visitor being in control? What would be his end-game? I began to wonder how he would react when his secret was finally revealed. What were his plans or me and our child?

In the midst of my pondering, my mind changed directions from Ben to my mother. My shame was enormous. I was so conflicted about whether or not to share this information with her. The verbal assault I launched on her vividly replayed in my mind. I remembered the pained look in her eyes. I didn't want her eyes or her words to add to the guilt I would be forced to endure. Big Mama once challenged me to keep living if I had not yet made any mistakes I regretted. Since that time, I had encountered many regrets. My pile continued to grow.

FIFTY-TWO

Exposed

My heartbeat quickened when I heard the keys jingling in the door. I fidgeted with my clothes and hair. I wondered if Ben would be able to see how much I had changed overnight. I possessed more strength than I realized. I had summoned the courage to walk away because I understood how powerful I had become. Those thoughts inspired me as I moved closer to my first honest glance at the father of my child.

When Ben walked through the door, the first words out of his mouth were "hey baby". I cringed at his salutation, the same as I did last night. My mind got stuck on his choice of words and I missed most of his initial conversation. My attention was lured away by curiosity. I looked closely at his left hand, trying to find any indication that a wedding band had occupied that reserved space. I saw nothing but the unblemished continuation of the skin attached to the hands of a man who brought me joy and at times, greater pain. But those hands would no longer be allowed to roam the hills and valleys of my body in search of sacred hollows. I feared my skin would scream if I allowed any physical connection with that married man. I accepted the fact that his last caress had been his final curtain call before our union faded to black.

I returned my attention to his face and tried to absorb the words Ben was intent on sharing. His mouth was moving, but I didn't internalize any of his words. His voice was too normal and his mood too pleasant for someone who harbored such despicable lies and unmeasurable dishonesty. No matter what phrases came from his mouth, my ears only heard the voice of deceit from someone whose aura was tarnished by the truth.

I knew it was inevitable, but I wasn't mentally prepared for the meeting of our eyes. I briefly searched his eyes for yesterday's innocence, but only saw last night's betrayal. After our eyes disconnected, I stared at his face. I wasn't sure who I was looking at. I wasn't sure I even knew his real name. I fought the urge to rub his face. I wanted to see if part of the mask he had been wearing since that day in the coffee shop would somehow rub off. I wanted to see the real person underneath the mask, but I realized it was his protection. It only allowed me to see what Ben wanted to reveal. I had trusted him above my mother. I would pay dearly for my unwise decision.

I tried to corral my feelings, but in the aftermath of his deceit, I lost control. Once I opened my mouth, the words flowed clearly and forcefully in his direction. "Why didn't you tell me you were married? Why didn't you let me choose whether or not I wanted to participate in adultery? How could you do this to me?"

His expression and his demeanor reeked of guilt. He

nervously chuckled and tried to avoid giving me a straight answer. "What makes you think I'm married? Have you been talking to your meddling mother again?"

"No, but I will be sure to call her after you leave. I am still waiting on an answer. Why didn't you tell me you were married?"

"Wow, I go out for twenty minutes and I return home to a crazy person. What's going on with you? Where is all of this coming from? Whoever is filling your head with the notion that I am married is a liar."

I audibly agreed. He stayed in denial until I recounted the side of the conversation I overheard. The surprised look on his face confirmed that the depth of my knowledge exceeded his forthrightness. My words were a gut check for him. The tension brewing within Ben became more evident. There was nothing he could say to negate my words. His lies had been exposed. We both knew it.

He attempted to move toward me, but no clear pathway existed. I had made a conscious effort to keep distance and obstacles between us as we continued to discuss his lies and my disappointment. The more I revealed, the more agitated Ben became. He cleared his throat to start an explanation, but I interrupted his train of thought with more of my authoritative stance. I made it abundantly clear that I no longer wanted to see his deceitful face. His place was with his wife and child. Whatever he wanted to tell them would be his decision. I had no intention of revealing any part of our liaison. It was not my truth to tell. He would have to find his own words. He would have to be responsible for announcing the destruction of his own family.

I said my peace and demanded he leave my home immediately. He threw his hands up in submission, collected his belongings and started walking toward my door for the last time. I wanted to tell him that the only communication he would ever get from me again would be from my attorney. He had earned the right to pay child support and I would be honored to help him fulfill his obligation. But those thoughts remained entombed in my mind. I concluded it would be wise to avoid that topic until later, if I wanted any chance of getting him out of my home for good.

Accepting the fact that he would be walking out of my door for the last time was harder than I wanted to admit. We had made so many plans that were worth no more than the breath of air it took to spill those sounds into the universe. The foundation I thought I was standing on took on the consistency of quicksand. I sank under the weight of unattainable aspirations. He was going back to his happy home. I would be left to pick up the pieces of my fractured life and try to move forward. It seemed unfair that he was getting a free pass without having to face any immediate consequences. I was sure that when he closed that door behind him, both my child and I would be as insignificant as the crumbs that fell onto the floor from last week's meal. No one appreciated that those small pieces had been part of something whole. Last night I decided against harming him physically. Instead, I opted to attack him mentally.

I knew I had gone too far when I told him, "You are nothing but a pathetic, adulterous, coward. I look forward to the day your child calls some other man daddy."

When Ben turned around and faced me, I saw the evil from his soul spilling out through his eyes. He was enraged. His body language and the anger etched on his face caused me to question my safety.

FIFTY-THREE

Trapped

When Ben made the sudden movement toward me, I knew he was about to cross a line that would not end well for any of us. I had two choices...run or run faster. I chose the latter. My attempts were thwarted by the depths of his contempt for me and his desire to punish me for my maternal arrogance. I felt like the mouse being toyed with by a not so playful cat whose intentions were less than prosperous for the prey. His physical body and his rage stood between me and freedom. I realized we were both trapped; he in his lies with me standing in his way and me in my date with destiny.

The first blow he landed across my face was enough to get his point across, but clearly he thought otherwise. He continued to inflict his punishment on my fragile gestational body. I could feel and hear the cracking of my bones as the full force of his fist made contact with my face. I stumbled backward in response to the next blow. The blood that filled my mouth breached one of its corners. It found its way onto the floor and against the wall. My legs tried to stay strong, but retreated in their effort to keep me standing. I fell violently to the floor like a rag doll. I wanted to plead for my life and the life of our child, but I was unwilling to give him that satisfaction. I prepared myself for the next blow. I knew I was out of natural options for escape. In desperation, I prayed for a force field to magically appear and protect me and my baby; anything to bring me some relief and to make this attack end.

The hope of having that prayer answered evaporated with the next kick to my lower back. A numbing pain claimed its place in my body. Somehow, in the midst of all that was going on, my only thoughts were to protect my child. With all that I had, I was willing to protect that life with mine. Maybe I would find redemption in the next life by allowing the world to experience the treasure I sheltered from harm. I had wished many times that my first child would never see the light of day and fate sided with me. Maybe it would be in my corner again as I sought to have the opportunity to groom this one for greatness.

I learned from my first attacker that power was their ultimate weapon. Stillness became my ally. As hard as it was to accomplish, the next blow garnered no reaction beyond the physical movements brought about by gravity. I had learned well to fake being asleep while at Big Mama's. I hoped Ben could be deceived as craftily as he had been earlier. Our lives depended on it. The walls reverberated with no whimper, no reaction, and no sound, except those made by him, evidenced by the sounds of extreme effort escaping his throat as his foot landed another powerful blow. Then, it was over. He believed he had conquered my physical body. He stood over me admiring his handiwork as he struggled to bring his breathing under control. I kept waiting for the sound of the squeaky hinges to indicate his departure as his footsteps moved away from me and closer to the door. The footsteps stopped, but unexpectedly changed direction. Their cadence quickened as they headed back toward me. My mind rapidly tried to find a scenario that would coincide with those facts. I tried to prepare myself for what was next. In a moment of temporary insanity, I wanted to believe that maybe his fit of rage was over and out of remorse, he was coming back to help me. He didn't rescue me. He kicked me again as hard as he could in my stomach. Because I had instinctively retreated into myself using the fetal position, I was able to partially shield my midsection with my arm. My entire body dislodged from its previous position and marked its new territory with my motionless form. My body surrendered, even though I had no white flag to wave. I fought to conceal my consciousness and control the human urge to cry out in pain. I didn't move, but the baby did. It let me know that its life continued despite the efforts of its father. At least one of us could rejoice. Then, as calmly as Ben entered the apartment, he left. The door shut and the lock clicked. He was really gone. He had completed his cowardly task. The condition of my body provided the evidence of the finality of his purpose. He was in search of his freedom. After all, he had an anniversary celebration with his wife to attend.

My tears quickly found their escape route. I let them have their way. I cried for many reasons while I lay there in my pool of hurt. I didn't know if Ben intended to kill me, but his actions and his centered attack confirmed to me that, one way or another, he did not want our baby to experience the external side of life. The unexpected revelation of his true intentions crushed pieces of my soul. I thought I knew him; that he was the one, but I had only been exposed to the candy coated shell that sweetly covered the nut at the center.

FIFTY-FOUR

Lifeline

I didn't know consciousness had abandoned me until it returned. With it came bewilderment, confusion and excruciating pain. I was unsure how long it had been since Ben had launched his cowardly assault on us. The shadows of twilight overtook the brightness of day. My vision was blurry, but my body was able to point out his places of triumph. I was afraid to move from the spot on the floor where I landed. Out of fear that another assault could be imminent, I remained silent and still for a bit longer. I strained my senses in an attempt to detect his presence. I was not sure if I was alone in the room or if he was waiting to see if round two of my punishment was necessary.

The stillness of the room greeted memories of my past. I thought about the quiet times spent on the porch swing with Big Mama, the sounds of her laughter, the gentleness of her touch and the love and safety I found in her arms. Those were truly peaceful times. How I wished my body and my mind could travel back to my childhood summer retreat. But I was firmly rooted in the now and with it came the recollection of the horrific trauma I recently experienced. Each labored breath allowed me to feel the throbbing pain that rippled through my body. I didn't want to move. I feared each small movement would be accompanied by an unending barrage of pain and agony. It would be so easy to just lay there and not have to move, but the possibility of survival diminished considerably using that logic. I had fought hard to survive, but maybe it was time to accept the inescapable conclusion of my and my baby's existence.

I allowed my mind to drift, not focusing on anything specific, just wanting to find some peace. I was sure that because of the trauma I recently sustained, the baby couldn't still be alive. And if that was true, I would undoubtedly travel that same path. I was content to prepare myself for the inevitable to come. I wanted to leave this side with my mind in a good place. Not thinking of the bad that had beset my life, but of all the good I experienced and the lessons I learned along the way. I admittedly had spent too many days of my life angry. I missed out on so much love because of my unwillingness to forgive. I overlooked the love I had, in search of the love I thought I needed. Somehow, I managed to miss out on both.

Until that time, I had never really understood or appreciated the love of a parent. I marveled at how vehemently I had fought to sustain the life that was inside me, even though our eyes had never met and our skin had never touched. Because I loved it so fiercely, I had been willing to give up my life for my child's, even without being asked. I couldn't imagine how much both my parents and my grandparents had loved me. The sacrifices they unselfishly made on my behalf had been more than my adolescent mind could comprehend. It had only demonstrated a fraction of their true devotion. I was lucky to have been loved by so many, when there are others who had never experienced love at all. In my mind, I wanted to be on that porch swing thinking of the things that gave me joy. I reminisced about the sounds of the crickets and the frogs, the feel of the summer breeze on my face, the lure of the green tomatoes that always made me sick, the smell of line-dried sheets, the futile attempt to grasp the smoke rings from my grandfather's pipe and rocking back and forth on that seat with my Big Mama. Those were the times I cherished the most. The purity of those moments was the thing I desired to be my last memories as my life came to its end.

I felt it wouldn't be long before I could be with Big Daddy, Big Mama and my father again. I would finally be able to meet my babies. I was sure I was closer than ever before when I began to hear Big Mama's voice. But how could that be? I could still feel pain. In eternity, there is no pain. My mind and body couldn't be in two dimensions at the same time. I wasn't sure if I was still awake or unconscious. Was it memories that caused my ears to entertain Big Mama's voice and hear the same calm instructions she had used many times before? I thought I heard her say, "It's time to get up baby."

She always called me a sleepy head because I hated to get up in the morning, especially on Sundays. Consequently, she often had to help start my day by gently nudging me into the morning. I would lie there in defiance until she made a second and sometimes a third trip, each time elevating the sternness of her instructions until she got the desired results. I kept trying to get my brain to catch up to reality so I could determine if I was fully awake. Then I heard her again.

"It's time to get up baby. You've got to fight hard for both of your lives. I'll stay right here with you."

"I can't Big Mama. It hurts too much right now and I am so tired." I just want us to come be with you."

"But you can't right now. It's not time. For the last time, I'm telling you to GET UP!"

"Yes, ma'am", was the only response I could give.

Somewhere in the distance, I heard the phone ringing. That sound became my lifeline. It gave me hope and something to concentrate on as a way out of my cocoon of suffering. If I could just get to the phone in time, this would be over. There would be no point in trying to stand. My feeble legs would not support such an effort. The constant battering to my back left my legs able to only feel slight tingling sensations. Besides, one of my eyes was nearly swollen shut and my vision in the other was completely gone. My only option was to drag myself over to the phone, hoping to find deliverance on the other end. Not far into my journey, I felt the new warmth of liquid escaping from my body. I had experienced this feeling in my past attempts at motherhood. I instinctively knew that my joy was in distress. The urgency of my situation had heightened significantly. I had to get to that phone. Time was becoming my subtle enemy.

Doubt strolled boldly into my thoughts and tried to convince me that my plan was pointless. I didn't allow it to linger long enough for me to stop fighting for our lives. With everything I had, I continued to pull my body with newfound purpose, leaving a trail of blood and determination behind me until I reached my destination. On the other end of the line I heard the voice of my mother. All I could manage to say was "Mama" before I dropped the phone in total exhaustion and relief. Finally, my body allowed itself to rest in triumph. An unexpected calmness quieted my mind and I managed to bring my breathing under control. Each time I inhaled, I was greeted with air saturated with the comforting smell of coffee. Big Mama had kept her promise.

FIFTY-FIVE

Recovery

The incessant beeping noise penetrated my uncon-sciousness and caused my mind to become entranced by its source. The longer I focused on the sound, the loud-er it became until my mind acknowledged my surround-ings. I was no longer on the floor of my home. I was in the sterile confines of a hospital room. My existence was being measured in consecutive beeps coming from a mechanical expression of life. I was overjoyed with the realization that we had survived that brutal attack. My joy was overturned when I moved and was beset with memories of the agony that accompanied Ben's rage. I had walked thru hell's half acre and I would carry the scars to prove it. There were no mirrors readily available to me, but the inability to open one eye let me know that glamour shots would not be on my to-do list anytime soon.

The attack had been brutal. I ached both inside and out. In the blink of an eye, my entire life had changed course. Once again, I would have to make peace with who I had become, after I figured that out. I never wanted to think that this was what I deserved, but when I thought about what I had endured, I was angry with myself. I threw a match on an unexposed combustible container; it exploded. I had leveraged my safety for a show of strength. It nearly cost us our lives. What armpit of the world did this person crawl from where it was acceptable to beat a woman within an inch of her life and leave her and their unborn child for dead? I was not sure where Ben came from, but I knew where he was going before he went to hell...jail.

I wanted to celebrate this victory with my baby. I habitually reached to caress my protruding stomach, only to find it gone. Since I began to provide shelter for that treasure, I had one job; to protect my child. Again, I had failed to sustain a life. After all the fighting and suffering, I had no evidence of the object of my fervent struggle; the reason behind my desperation. I wanted so much to be a mother and once again, I would be unable to claim that title. My baby was gone. It had been a byproduct of the sponsor of alternative facts and Ben had taken back what he couldn't control. Some say you can't miss what you've never had. As the person doing without, I could refute that myth. My child was just within my reach the last time I closed my eyes. My life continued, but not my child's. Was this my penance for the way I had treated my first child, my Big Mama and my mother? I still had not earned the right to be a mother. Apparently I had not convinced the universe that I was worthy enough to receive the gift of the unconditional seeds of love that are planted with every conception. I would have to use the "what ifs" to substitute for unfulfilled longings.

A warm river of tears slowly meandered from my lids and lubricated the hollows of my ears before being gobbled up by the pools at the bottom of my neck. How morbidly conflicting I found my familiar friends. My tears had been a constant reminder of all my failures, broken promises and hopes. Remembering all the reasons our paths crossed, I asked myself what good could come from my survival and my child's demise. I had no answer that would justify my loss. The tears formed an alliance with shrieks of anguish and caused my body to react with uncontrollable violent movements. The more hysterical I became, the quicker the beeping sound registered on the life-counting monitor. The drugs that were administered calmed me enough to stop the hysterical crying, but it only provided a short-term solution. Each time I became aware of my surroundings, I signaled the need for more pharmaceutical relief until my body succumbed to the stillness caused by an unconscious mind.

Eventually, not even those man-made narcotic detours could block out the relentless storms brewing in my mind. I was forced to feel the pain that would guide me to self-truth. As I lay flat on my back in that hospital bed, I had to stand in my truth about the decisions and mistakes in my own life. There was nowhere to run. I learned a long time ago that feeling sorry for myself accomplished nothing; it just kept me stuck in a place I didn't want to be. But just for that day, I wanted to wallow in the self-pity I had earned.

The pivotal moments of my life swarmed around in my mind. I tried to find planes of discovery based on my map of the world. Just like everyone else, I needed to feel as if I really mattered. As humans, we often walk over each other to have our abstract sense of validation fulfilled. Very rarely do we realize how fleeting that mission can be. Each time the satisfaction quotient gets close to being realized, the target moves a bit further beyond our reach. I kept looking for something or someone external to make me happy. I never wanted to acknowledge my contribution to a distorted version of truths that negatively impacted my life. I avoided the obvious.

After my father died, my life had been like the ocean waves; always in a hurry to get somewhere, but never staying long before cresting, retreating and heading for the next destination. Often the new shoreline ended up being no better than the previous one, once the fragments of things caught up beneath the surface were left behind. The waves could be calming and appealing to the senses, while hiding wreckage that was always willing to be resurrected. I thought that if I kept moving fast enough, my past would not be able to catch up to me. I would be happy before it noticed. But, after I stood over the bed of a sleeping human with a knife in my hand and confusion in my eyes, I knew I would never be able to outrun who was living inside me. I had to accept who and what I was. Then I had to work on finding the pieces of the puzzle that were missing.

The first place I looked was within. I saw things that had caused great turmoil for me. At times I felt like a rock in someone's shoe that, once discovered, was cast aside as an annoyance. Who could sustain self-esteem and recognition of who they were under those circumstances; if seldom in their life they felt like a precious stone? I released healing water for the girl who had been locked up for so long, being held hostage by my past; the one who had been left behind; the one who had been raped; the one who had hidden a secret pregnancy; the one whose first true love betrayed her; the one who traded her body for the notion of love; the one who had forgotten to love herself first; the little girl who wanted nothing more than to be with her mother. All those things had been the ransom for the freedom I had been seeking, but none of those truly defined who I was destined to become. In the grand scheme of my life, those trappings would merely be a footnote in the complete story of me. They were just fragments of my past and I was ready and willing to cast off those bindings so that I could reveal the person I was meant to be.

Behavior doesn't immediately change the heart, but it's the place to start. I kept repeating the same patterns, hoping for a different outcome. But that vortex of irrationality was about to end. I knew I wouldn't be able to change overnight, but it was time for a transformation that began and ended with me. I had to learn to discover my true self at my own pace. I always thought something was missing from my life and I was right. I had been missing, but I was determined to have a presence in my own life. I was better than the habits I had exhibited. I owed it to the people who had sacrificed so much for me to do better.

I began to realize that what we accept is often tainted by what we feel. The life I wanted and thought I deserved may not ever materialize. I had to be willing to let go of everything that stood in the way of making me feel whole. Fighting to hold on to those dreams had only steered me down a path of destruction; so much so that I had slept with danger and almost didn't wake up. I had not known who I was apart from my trying to reach a goal that kept moving beyond my grasp. How much longer would I force my life to crumble under the weight associated with my overbearing hunger? I wasn't sure what the answer was to that question, but eventually my life would come together when I was ready. My immediate emphasis had to be on healing my broken body; the mental aspects would take a bit longer. At the end of my conversation with myself, I felt liberated by self-discovery and calmness lingered long enough for sleep to once again overtake my mind.

FIFTY-SIX

Finding Joy

My mother was sitting right beside my bed when I next opened my eyes. Her worried smile greeted me. The look of concern remained evident as she stood over me and gently caressed my face. "I thought I had lost you again", was all she could say before she released her tears. The sorrowful droplets burned with love as they touched my face. I could not hold back my emotions. The grief associated with the loss of another war with nature trickled out.

My mother had a puzzled look on her face as I blubbered unrecognizable syllables that only I could understand about the tragic loss of my child. The more I tried to express my feelings, the more inconsolable I became. All she could do was hold me tightly as she kept repeating the word "no" while I kept clutching her and shaking my head "yes". I vividly recalled the feelings of helplessness in those moments when I begged Big Mama to get my love child back. It appeared my history of loss had repeated itself. I knew better than to harbor pointless aspirations when faced with the certainty of my loss. My mother allowed my hysteria to run its course before shocking me back into my senses. "It's gonna be ok." You both are gonna be ok. I just saw my grandbaby. She's beautiful."

It took a moment for me to totally comprehend my mother's words. But when I did, the tears of pain changed identity midstream. They became tears of joy, sprinkled with relief. I continued to shelter myself in the bosom of my mother and started to laugh and cry at the same time. How unbelievable that life's miracle had remained long enough for me to earn the privilege of being called a mother. More than anything, I wanted to know and feel that I really mattered in this life. I believed it now and was willing to work harder for my child than for anything else I had ever done. So much love had been stored up from maternal disappointments. I was ready to pour the entire reservoir into my tiny miracle. She had fought the battle with me and I couldn't wait for us to finally meet.

I felt as though my heart would explode from happiness when my one functioning eye was treated to an unobstructed vision of my dream. Peering through the window into the face of love filled me with a contentment that was like salve being rubbed over unhealed wounds. Layers of hurt and disappointment began to fall away. After each joy-filled blink, hope and wonderment permeated my heart with the same love and maternal desire that sprang up in me many lost years ago. I was in awe of the continuation of life that had detached itself from my core and was still within reach. That was a first for me. The longer I looked at her face, the more grateful I became for the determination I had exhibited during my fight for her existence. I realized how close I had come to giving in to doubt. I would have missed out on this miracle. The pain and the sacrifices associated with that battle for her life were quickly forgotten with each tiny breath she took. She looked fragile to many, but I knew she was a fighter. She had reminded me to fight when I needed to be encouraged the most. I instinctively reached forward to touch her, but the unsympathetic window pane prevented the transfer of my heart to hers through physical currents that could only be manifested by human touch. My eyes would have to hold her until my hands would not threaten her sterile existence.

My mother stepped away from the wheelchair and allowed me to have my bonding moment with my child. This was truly the most beautiful sight in the entire world. She made me proud to be her mother. Just when I thought my love for her had reached its apex, space in my heart opened up and made room for more. With the purity of this new love came the unquenchable hunger to feast on these maternal feelings to my heart's desire. I fought with the devil to sustain her life and I would allow that pride to raise my head and puff out my chest, just a little. Because of my unaccomplished births, I would never take her for granted. I knew this bundle would not be responsible for my happiness; that was left up to me. Her job would be to allow me to love her as hard as humanly possible. That expression of unconditional love would help dry up jars of tears I had filled up in the wake of life's disappointments.

Although I had been mesmerized by these new beginnings, I knew I hadn't gotten there alone. Generations of love converged in the space between each tiny heartbeat. Had it not been for Big Mama's wisdom and guidance, we would not have been able to feast on this tiny existence. I was so fortunate my mother had been there to save us. I reached